KATIE

CLOVER SPRINGS MAIL ORDER BRIDES 1

RACHEL WESSON

LONDONGATE PUBLISHING

CHAPTER 1

BOSTON 1880

A bell clanged loudly before the hold doors were opened. Katie closed her eyes tightly as the blinding sunlight lit up the dark interior of the ship's hold. She tensed, as the heavy footsteps got louder, wrapping her arm protectively around Ellen's shoulders. The younger girl snuggled closer to her.

"We have arrived in American waters and will dock in Boston later today." The ship's captain looked around him, holding a handkerchief to his nose. "Before you will be allowed to disembark and start your new lives in America, every passenger must pass a medical inspection. The doctor and his team will visit shortly. Clean up this pigsty you have called home for the last five weeks."

The crowd surged forward, unhappy with the

captain's comments. Despite people muttering, nobody confronted the captain directly, but perhaps sensing the angry mood, he left quickly.

"He must think we wanted to live in this filth," Mary Ryan tutted angrily as she surveyed the scene around her. "How many times have we asked—no, begged—for hot water for washing and cleaning?"

Katie shook her head. She didn't want to dwell on the horrible journey. There was no point in wasting energy on things that couldn't be changed. "Come on, Mary, get a hold of yourself. You heard the captain. If we don't pass that inspection, what will they do with us?"

"It will be the workhouse."

Katie looked at the old woman who had spoken. The workhouse. That word put the fear of God into all of the passengers. Everyone knew some poor unfortunate soul who had ended up in one of those places back home. Katie pulled her shoulders back and put her chin up. She hadn't come all this way to end up in a workhouse. They had come to America to seek their fortune, and nothing was going to stop them from succeeding. Doctor or not, they were getting off this stinking ship.

"We won't be going to the workhouse, will we, Katie?" Ellen's pinched white face looked up at Katie, her eyes filled with terror. "Daddy said Uncle Joe would be waiting for us to take us to his nice house."

"Of course he will, Ellen, me darling. When did Daddy ever lie?"

"You are so lucky. The two of you will be set up for life." Mary looked away, but not before Katie saw the jealousy in her face. "Catherine and I haven't got any family. It's just the two of us, but we will be fine. They say the roads are paved with gold in America."

Katie couldn't stop herself from giving Mary a hug. The Ryan girls had helped make the horrible journey a bit more pleasant. Both were hard working, respectable girls whose family had taken advantage of the assistance package offered by Irish landlords to those who wanted to emigrate to America.

Well, *wanted* was putting it a bit strongly. When there was nothing left but cold, hunger and certain death in the country of your birth, wouldn't anyone with a brain take the chance to go to America? Katie didn't believe the streets were paved with gold, but there was a chance of a new life. As Mam used to say, if you worked hard and stayed honest and respectable, the good Lord would provide success.

Katie closed her eyes. She couldn't reconcile the good Lord with the filth and tragedy they'd had to endure in the last few weeks. If prayers were enough, everyone who had boarded the ship would arrive fit and healthy in the land of their dreams. Instead, Mary and Catherine had to watch as their daddy, Mam and little sister had been buried at sea, only three of the many victims of the horrible trip.

Four sailors climbing down the ladder brought Katie back to the present. They ordered the passengers to bundle up the old blankets and rags they had slept on. Despite some protests from the older women, the sailors grabbed these bundles and took them up to the deck to dump into the ocean. They returned to scrape together all the moldy hay and other dirt that had accumulated over the last five weeks and this, too, was bundled together for disposal over the side. Numerous buckets of scalding hot water and some carbolic soap were then lowered into the hold with instructions for the women and children to scrub themselves clean.

Despite the too-hot water, Katie wished she could insert her whole body into the bucket. She longed to be fully clean. Instead, she settled for a quick wash, including her hair. Once she was finished, she helped Ellen wash before assisting some of the other passengers with the younger children. Once everyone had washed up, the dirty water was used to scrub the floors and wooden bunks.

All too soon, the doctor and his team arrived. As

Katie, Ellen, Mary and Catherine waited their turn, they watched in horror as the team sent one family after another to the line for the hospital.

"Pinch your cheeks, girls, and stand straighter. If he asks if you have had a fever or a cough, say no," Katie whispered as the line in front of them moved forward. "And for goodness sake, don't you dare start coughing, Ellen, me darling."

Ellen's lips moved. Katie guessed her younger sister was praying. She kept her fingers crossed as their turn arrived.

"Name and age?" the doctor asked as he gave Katie the once-over.

"Kathleen O'Callaghan. Seventeen years of age. This is my younger sister, Ellen. She's twelve."

"Is she simple? Do you have to speak for her?"

"No, of course not." Katie's indignant tone rang clear. "She's not used to strangers, that's all." Katie glared at Ellen, trying to make her sister understand she had to speak for herself. When that didn't work, she stamped on her sister's foot.

"Ouch. What did you do that for?" Ellen's angry voice made the doctor smile.

"Move along, girls. Nothing ailing you that a couple of weeks in the sunshine won't clear up. Welcome to America."

Katie grabbed Ellen's arm and pushed her in front

of her. She wasn't taking any chances on Ellen coughing and causing the doctor to change his mind. To her relief, Mary and Catherine also passed the inspection.

The four girls clasped hands as they waited on deck looking at the first sight of America. Katie gulped deep breathes of salty sea air. It was almost enough to remove the stench of rotting hay and stale sweat that had assailed their nostrils during the long trip.

She looked around her, curious to see what their new home would be like. They had sailed into the East Bay and all around them ships jostled for position, some landing like theirs and others heading back to sea. Katie crossed herself, thanking God she wasn't going out on that ocean. Once she got on dry land, nothing and nobody would make her set foot on a ship ever again.

"Where are you going to go?" Katie asked Mary. "If you want to stay with us, I can ask Uncle Joe to help you and Catherine get settled. I am sure he wouldn't leave you alone in a new city." Katie wasn't sure of anything, never having met Uncle Joe, but he was daddy's brother. Daddy wouldn't leave two women alone to fend for themselves, never mind two girls younger than her. His brother was likely to be of the same mind. Wasn't he?

Uncertainty clouded Mary Ryan's face. "Do you really think so, Katie? If it was just me, I would find a place quickly, but with Catherine to look after, too..." Her friend's voice trailed off, unshed tears making her voice husky.

"You must stay with us and that's final. I promised your Mam, God rest her, that I would help you. Katie O'Callaghan never breaks her word." The port was busy. Hooves clattered on the cobblestones, relatives shrieked to claim lost family members, and everyone seemed to be in a hurry while they waited.

Katie looked around for somewhere to stand away from the jostling crowds but not too far that her uncle wouldn't spot them. "Let's wait over there. It's a bit quieter."

"What are those youngsters doing? One of them is going to be killed." Mary said, pointing at some ten-year-old boys who were weaving in and out of the new arrivals.

"Someone on board said they were runners. Their job is to take your bags so you have to stay in a certain lodging house. The owners of the lodging houses pay them to find customers."

The girls watched as the young boys darted forward and back, sometimes getting in arguments with reluctant passengers. Several times, the boys were clouted for their efforts but still they persisted until the main body of passengers had departed. A couple of the runners eyed the four girls as they stood waiting, but Katie's glare was sufficient for the boys not to disturb them. For now.

CHAPTER 2

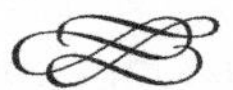

"What does Uncle Joseph look like, Katie?" Ellen bit her lip, looking around the busy port.

Katie took her sister's hand. "Stop fretting, Ellen. We'll find him. Just keep your eyes out for a man who looks like Daddy."

Katie hoped she sounded more confident than she felt. Despite being on dry land, her body still felt like it was moving to the roll of the ocean waves. Her stomach rose as another bout of nausea hit her. Her whole body screamed for rest and the last thing she wanted to do was stand in a busy port waiting for an uncle she didn't know.

Daddy had written to Uncle Joe, thanking him for the tickets and confirming their date of arrival. *Maybe he didn't get the letter.* Katie almost believed that until

Ellen poked her in the ribs. She followed her sister's gaze, swallowing hard. The tall, slim gentleman was the image of Daddy. Well, what Daddy would look like if he had new clothes and enough to eat.

Although staring was rude, Katie couldn't speak. She kept swallowing to get rid of the lump in her throat. Then she looked at his face and all resemblance to Daddy ended. Her father's eyes had always shone with love and happiness whenever he looked at his girls. Katie pulled Ellen closer as she instinctively shrank back from the look in the cold blue eyes staring back at her.

The minutes passed and the silence grew uncomfortable. *He is waiting for me to say something.* Katie let Ellen's hand fall and rubbed her palm on her dress before offering it to her uncle.

"Hello, Uncle Joe, I'm Katie and this is Ellen. These two other girls are friends from home. Mary and Catherine Ryan. Their parents died on the trip over," she stammered, as his disdainful gaze traveled from the top of her head to her feet and back to her face.

"My name is Joseph, but you, young lady, can call me Sir. Couldn't you have found better clothes to wear?"

Katie felt Ellen shaking beside her. She grabbed her sister's hand and stood straighter. Mam had always told them to stand tall and be proud of who they were and where they came from. In the voice she reserved for the nuns at school and imagining she wore the type of dress favored by rich ladies, Katie answered.

"These are our Sunday dresses. I understand they may look a little worn, but it was a long, rough crossing."

What had he expected? It wasn't that long ago since he had left Ireland. Didn't he remember the conditions on board the ship? Obviously not, judging by the way he made sure not to touch either of them.

"Pick up your bag and follow me. I have arranged for your other luggage to be taken care of." Her uncle marched off toward a small buggy. All four girls followed in his wake, but after a couple of steps, her uncle turned around. He pointed at his nieces. "You girls get up in the buggy."

He turned his attention to the Ryan girls. "My niece was wrong to give you the impression I pick up waifs and strays. There is a convent at the top of that street. I am sure the good sisters will make use of two more pair of hands."

Katie couldn't believe it. He was going to let the youngsters fend for themselves in a new country. Daddy would turn in his own grave before he would be that callous.

"Please, Uncle—I mean Sir. I promised Mrs. Ryan I would help Mary look after Catherine. She hasn't been too well, but nothing a warm bed and some hot food wouldn't cure." Katie stopped talking at the look her uncle gave her.

"Lesson learned, young lady. You have no business making promises you can't keep. Now get up on the buggy with your sister, or perhaps you would prefer to accompany your friends to the convent?"

At the obvious threat, Katie gave Mary a look of apology and moved toward the buggy. If she had been alone, she would have told her uncle to get lost, but she had to think of Ellen.

"Go on, Katie. We will be fine. If the sisters are renowned for their charity, God will look after us all." Mary Ryan waved goodbye before taking Catherine's hand and walking in the direction of the convent. Katie stared at her friends' departing figures until she lost sight of them.

I swear I will find a way to help you, Mary Ryan, so help me I will.

CHAPTER 3

Ellen looked terrified, so Katie held her hand tightly for the short trip back to their uncle's home.

She looked around at the pretty houses lining their route. Some were bigger than others, but even the smallest was much larger than their old home. When her uncle pulled up outside one house, Katie prayed her aunt was nicer than the stranger beside them.

When they went inside the house, they didn't have a chance to look around as a servant waited to greet them.

"Nellie, these are my nieces. As you can see, they both need a good wash and new clothes before they can meet the mistress. Burn the rags they are wearing."

Katie opened her mouth, but shut it again quickly at the look on her uncle's face. She looked at Nellie who returned her gaze, her eyes full of sympathy and understanding.

Nellie's kindness was nearly Katie's undoing. Angrily, she swiped the tears away from her eyes as she watched the older woman help Ellen wash and braid her hair. Katie longed to ask her questions, but the magic of soaking in hot water after weeks at sea took over.

All too soon they were washed, dressed in new clothes and ready to be presented to their aunt. Katie hoped her stomach wouldn't grumble. They were starving, but it seemed food had to wait until later.

Nellie escorted them to meet their aunt. They walked through the richly furnished house, their bare feet sinking into deep carpet. When they got to the door of the sitting room, Nellie knocked before whispering.

"Whatever you do, don't answer the mistress back. She don't like to be crossed."

Katie didn't have a chance to answer as Nellie pushed them both into the room, closing the door behind them.

Their uncle was standing by a chair, his wife sitting straight-backed on the sofa.

"Kathleen and Ellen, this is your Aunt Margaret. She isn't feeling too well and will need your help to run our household."

He looked at them expectantly. Katie swallowed. "Yes, Uncle. I mean Sir."

"Thank you, Kathleen. I will leave my wife to inform you of your duties. I have to go out."

"Not again, Joseph." Margaret put her hand up as if to grasp her husband's hand, but he brushed her aside. The look he gave his wife was enough for all three to fall silent and gaze at the floor as he stalked out of the room.

Katie risked a glance at the lady sitting on the sofa, expecting to see tears. The eyes staring back at her were full of hatred. Katie took a step back.

"Your uncle insisted that we do our Christian duty and provide you with a home here in Boston, but believe me I will not stand by and watch you being idle. You may be used to sitting around all day back home in Ireland, but here you will work for your keep. So far, we have spent a fortune to bring you girls here. It would have been more economical to employ local staff, Lord knows, but if it is one thing Boston is not short of, it's work-shy immigrants."

Katie opened her mouth to speak but decided against it. It wouldn't do to antagonize the woman, not when they didn't have anywhere else to go.

"The devil makes work for idle hands. I expect you to work hard, keep yourselves clean and chaste, and above all, do nothing to damage your uncle's reputation. Do I make myself clear?"

The girls nodded in response, Ellen slipping her hand into Katie's.

"When I ask you a question, I expect an answer. I won't stand for any insolence or bad manners in my home. Now you, girl, ring that bell."

Katie did as instructed and soon there was a knock, the door opened and Nellie came in.

"You called, Ma'am."

"Nellie, these girls are here to help you. Show them to their room and tomorrow you can instruct them on their new tasks. Good night, girls."

Their aunt turned away. Katie squeezed Ellen's hand reassuringly before saying to her aunt's back, "Thank you very much, Aunt Margaret, for bringing us to America. We will work hard. Daddy and Mam brought us up proper. We know how to behave."

Her aunt whirled around, eyes fiery with temper.

"Obviously, you don't. The word is *properly,* not *proper,* and if that were the case, you would know not to speak to your betters. Here, girl, you speak only when spoken to. Now leave." Margaret turned her back and walked toward the chair where her husband had stood earlier.

Katie opened her mouth, but Nellie grabbed her

arm, shaking her head quickly. She motioned at the girls to follow her.

"Goodnight, Ma'am."

The cook closed the door behind them, crossing herself as she mumbled something.

"Don't go upsetting the mistress. She will make you pay in ways you can only imagine. Before you go to bed, come down to the kitchen for a quick bite to eat. I'm guessing you are hungry. The master is out for the evening and she will stay where she is for a while yet."

Katie and Ellen followed the cook gratefully back to the kitchen. They were starving and the aroma of fresh baking teased their senses.

Ellen started eating right away. Katie took her seat, but before she lifted her fork, she asked Nellie if she knew of a convent near the port.

"That would be St. Margaret's, the orphanage run by the Sisters of Mercy. Although why they are called that is anyone's guess." Nellie's face screwed up in distaste. "Why are you asking me, child?"

"We had some friends on board the ship. Their parents died during the crossing. I thought Uncle Joseph would help them." Katie couldn't say anything else. Her voice felt strangled.

"Your uncle sent them to the sisters? That would be about right. I am not one to judge my betters, but when it comes to that man, he would give God a hard time to find anything decent about him."

Nellie shook her head. She wiped a tear from her eye with her apron before giving Katie a big hug.

"Don't you fret, Katie, my girl. You and your sister will both be fine here. Nellie will see to it. Just you wait and see. Now eat up while the food is still hot. Life is always better with a full belly."

"Thank you. These are delicious," Ellen said, in between mouthfuls of food.

"You never had flapjacks before?"

"Not like these." Ellen spoke with her mouth full but Katie was too tired to correct her.

Nellie beamed as Katie and Ellen showed their appreciation by clearing their plates. Katie watched without comment as Ellen used her finger to mop up the last traces of the syrup Nellie called molasses. *Maybe America won't be so bad after all. I will find the convent and give Mary our address. We can stay in contact by letter until the time comes when we can be together again.*

Nellie showed them to the cold attic room they were to share. There were two beds, but after quickly undressing, they both climbed into the same one.

"Katie, I want to go home. I don't like it here. It's not like Daddy promised," Ellen whispered, clutching Katie as if she would disappear in the night.

"Hush, Ellen darling. We are lucky. Imagine if we had to go to the nuns."

Katie's stomach turned when she saw the effect of her words on Ellen. Her job was to comfort her sister, not worry her. She pulled the girl closer. "Nellie seems very nice and kind. We got well fed, too. It will be much better in the morning with Aunt Margaret. You'll see. Now get some sleep."

Katie hoped Ellen would believe her, even if she had little faith in what she was saying. She held her sister close until her sobs gave way. The child had fallen asleep, her little face wet with tears. *We won't stay here long, my darling girl, I promise.*

But even as she promised, Katie's heart fell. They had only a few pennies left from the money Daddy had given her. That wouldn't be enough to get them away from Uncle Joseph and his horrible wife.

CHAPTER 4

The first two weeks passed quickly. The girls were exhausted. They were used to cleaning but nothing had prepared them for the amount of work required to please their aunt. Time after time, she reprimanded them for not meeting her standards. Usually Katie couldn't see what she was complaining about, but her aunt's sharp tongue meant she stayed quiet. Ellen lost her ability to smile and cried herself to sleep every night. Katie envied her sister's ability to rest. She couldn't relax, her mind spinning over and over, trying to find a way out of their present situation.

Katie stared at the ceiling. *Mam, we need your help.* Mam was dead; Daddy was thousands of miles away. Ellen was too young. It was up to her. She had to find a way out of this mess. She just had to.

Katie stretched and reluctantly left the warm bed calling Ellen to get dressed quickly. Today, they were to accompany their aunt and uncle to church for the first time.

Waves of homesickness swept over Katie, caused by the familiar smell of incense and the sound of the Latin Mass. Ellen spotted Mary and Catherine Ryan and pulled on Katie's dress, causing their aunt to reprimand them both for fidgeting.

Katie couldn't believe how awful little Catherine looked. The girl stared at her without any sign of recognition. Mary didn't wave, but instead looked nervously at the harsh-looking nun who was monitoring her every move.

Maybe we will get to speak at the end of service. It seemed unlikely they would get the chance, but then Uncle Joseph unknowingly came to the rescue. The nun in charge of Mary Ryan's group greeted Katie's uncle like a long lost friend. Thus, with their guardians otherwise engaged, the girls were able to catch up in excited whispers.

"What's it like in the convent?"

"Oh, Katie, it's awful. The only time we get to spend together is here at church. Catherine has to sew all day long in the orphanage. Look at her. She looks like she will keel over any second. I have to work in the kitchens. If I was on my own, I would run away, but I couldn't leave Catherine alone." Mary bit her lip.

Katie took her hand and gave it a squeeze. It wasn't much, but she didn't want anyone to see. "We will find a way out, Mary. Have faith."

"Faith? Honest to God, Katie, if you spent five minutes in the orphanage you wouldn't have any belief left. You should see how harshly the little ones are handled. I wish I could take each and every one away. But we have to be careful. The ones they don't like get sent on the orphan trains."

"The what?"

"Come along, girls. It's time to go home." Uncle Joseph looked at Katie and Ellen, his tone making sure they moved quickly.

"See you next week, Mary." Katie whispered, but there was no sign her friend heard her. She gripped Ellen's hand tightly as they turned to leave the church, but the priest stopped them by calling out to their uncle.

"Joseph O'Callaghan, 'tis lovely to see you and the wife. Are these fine girls your nieces come over from Galway?" The priest didn't give Joseph a chance to reply, but turned instead to Katie. "Father Molloy is my name, but sure you be knowing that. How was your trip over? It nearly killed me. I pray every day that our Holy Father doesn't see fit to send me back over the ocean again." Katie and Ellen giggled at the look on the kindly priest's face. "'Tis lovely to have a chance to speak to some of my own people. I am from a village called Monivea. It's a small place just outside Athenry. Do you know it?" The girls nodded. "Would you come to tea next Tuesday? I would be right glad of the company. I mightn't want to cross the sea, but I do get homesick for the old country."

Katie saw their uncle was going to decline on their behalf, so she answered quickly. "Thank you very much, Father. We would love to come. Mary Ryan might know people from your village. She lived further away from the city than we did. She and her little sister Catherine live in the orphanage. Their parents died on the voyage over."

Please invite them, too.

Father Molloy winked, before saying loudly, "I will ask Mother Superior to allow the Ryan girls to come to tea, too. Mrs. Raines, my housekeeper, will bake us a cake. We will have a feast." Father Molloy turned to Uncle Joseph. "It's a real pity you have to work, Joseph, or you would be welcome too. See you Tuesday, girls."

Katie tried her best to hide her smile as they left the church. Uncle Joseph looked like he had sucked a lemon, but even he wasn't brave enough to turn down an invitation from the priest.

Thank you, Mam. You sure work in mysterious ways. I

know we are luckier than most. It may not be luxurious at Uncle Joseph's house, but at least we are together. We have our health and Nellie to look after us.

CHAPTER 5

NEAR CLEAR CREEK, COLORADO

Montis Cassidy kicked off his spurs, taking his frustration at his brother out on the mongrel at his feet. *A wife.* What in hell's bells did he need one of those for? They had China George to cook for them, he took his laundry to old Mrs. Williams, and if he ever needed some company, there was the saloon.

Virgil was wrong. There was no need for a woman around here. Montis surveyed the room. It wasn't the cleanest he had seen, but they never had company, so what did it matter?

What was it Virgil had said? Having a wife would make him more respectable. *Respectable.* What good did that do? He'd rather have money in his pocket. He stalked over to the table, looking at the congealed mess sitting on the plate. He hurled it to the floor in frustration. He should have eaten in town. As he looked at the mess on the floor, his stomach rumbled. It sure would be good to have someone cook some decent food for a change. China George served beans with everything.

Montis scratched his beard. Might be nice to have someone to warm his bed. It got mighty cold during the winter months. Having someone to spend time with would make the long summer nights pass pleasantly enough, too. The grin on his face disappeared as he remembered the last woman to live in this house.

What if she's like Ma? No, there couldn't be anyone as bad as her. If he closed his eyes, he could still hear her screaming as she battered him with a skillet or whatever else came to hand. She had never hit Virgil, though. She left him for Pa to deal with.

His skin crawled as he thought he heard his brother ride up. It must be getting late if he was home. He looked out the window, but it was only one of the hands. He sighed with relief.

Virgil always got his own way. There was no use arguing, especially if his brother had stopped into the saloon before coming home. He might as well get on with it or he would risk another black eye or worse.

He sat back down at the table and licked the top of the pencil.

. . .

Wanted:

Pretty wife for medium sized prosperous ranch owner.

Montis stopped. That sounded good, didn't it? Okay, he had to write something about himself.

I'm 28 years old, got all my own teeth and brown hair. I'm 6ft and of slim build. I have myself some horses, cattle and other farm animals. Need wife who knows how to care for livestock. Looking for a first rate housekeeper and cook. Must be used to solitary life as nearest town is about two-hour drive away.

Further the better as far as Montis was concerned. Oh, best add something about going to church. What was it that the advert had mentioned? A reference from his minister.

The minister. Now, how would Virgil get around that one? Montis scratched his head with the pencil. He added a line at the end confirming he was a regular churchgoer and upstanding member of the local community.

He sat looking at the untidy piece of paper. No matter how hard he tried, his writing always looked as if there were spiders running loose. It would have to do.

Where was Virgil anyway? The door banged. *Speak of the devil.*

"Montis. You got that letter wrote yet? Or do I need to do it for you?"

"Why you so keen to see me get hitched? Why can't you get a wife if you want one so much?" Montis risked answering back. Virgil seemed in a better mood than usual.

"I am too old to be setting up home with some woman. But someone needs to. China George isn't getting any better at cooking and nobody coming here is ever going to believe we are respectable gentlemen."

Huh! We're not gentlemen, never mind respectable, and one woman's not going to change that. But Montis kept his thoughts to himself. There was no point in getting Virgil all riled up. He took the crumpled letter out of his pocket.

Maybe nobody would want to come out west. *Virgil couldn't force him to marry if a girl didn't show up.*

CHAPTER 6

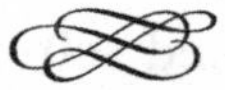

BOSTON

Boston Brides - Mail Order Bride Service

Seeks young women of good health, reputation and family background. Must be accomplished in domestic skills and keen to wed and make their home out West.

If interested, please reply, in strictest confidence, to Mrs. Maura Gantley of Boutwell Avenue, Train Street, Dorchester, enclosing a letter of introduction accompanied by two character references, one of which should be from your minister.

KATIE STARED at the advertisement in the *Boston Chronicle*. Could she marry a man she hadn't met? Her mother would turn in her grave. But what choice did she have? There weren't many positions open to unmarried Irish girls in the Boston area and even fewer still for those who insisted on bringing along their younger sister. *Wonder whether Mrs. Gantley would allow Ellen to accompany me?* Probably best not to mention her younger sister until a match had been agreed upon. Katie smiled self-consciously. She hadn't been accepted yet, but she was almost packing her battered old traveling trunk.

Could she live out West? Well, anything was preferable to staying under Aunt Margaret's roof for much longer. In her more Christian thoughts, she almost felt sorry for her childless aunt whose husband seemed to do his utmost to stay away from home. But having been on the receiving end of Margaret's temper, she understood Uncle Joseph's reluctance to seek out her company.

When she got married, she wouldn't give her husband reason to seek comfort elsewhere. She'd better stop thinking that way or she would spend hours on her knees saying rosaries, asking for forgiveness. Not that she could ever admit to Father Molloy she had been thinking about her future husband and their marriage bed. Cheeks hot, she shoved the ad in her pocket and started scrubbing the table so hard with the polishing cloth, she could have rubbed a hole in the wood.

As she got on with her chores, her mind explored

the potential pitfalls. *I wonder if Nellie knows of Mrs. Gantley.* Maybe she wasn't respectable. There were rumors of ladies who offered women *opportunities* not at all suitable for innocent young girls. Taking the paper out of her pocket, Katie read over the ad again. Surely the *Boston Chronicle* would check. Still best to talk to Nellie before she sent off her letter. Nellie would help with the character references. It wasn't as if she could ask Aunt Margaret to provide one. That old witch would destroy any hope of a happy future if she got the chance.

Would Father Molloy give her a character reference? She wasn't sure he would help her marry someone unless he was satisfied the gentleman was also a Catholic and willing to wed in church. *Perhaps he would give me one if I said it was for a job?*

Maybe Mrs. Gantley matches up couples on the basis of religious beliefs. Personally, she didn't care what religion the man was or whether they got married by a Judge or a priest. The events of the last year made her doubt the existence of the God everyone in her family seemed to have absolute faith in. Sure, she attended church and all the associated services, but that was for Ellen's benefit as well as an excuse to escape from her aunt's clutches for a few hours. Katie smirked. Father Molloy would tell Mrs. Gantley she was one of his most fervent believers, as she and Ellen went to as many prayer services as they could.

She liked the old priest and enjoyed the Tuesday evenings at his house. His housekeeper might not be as good a cook as Nellie but she was a kind old soul. She could see the Ryan girls were underfed and always had a feast waiting for them. Father Molloy got called away so regularly that the girls believed it was his way for them to get a chance to catch up with each other in private. Katie was grateful to the kind old man. She loved seeing her friends and it meant time away from Aunt Margaret.

Taking the ad back out of her pocket, she checked to see if anything about faith had been mentioned, though she knew well what the words said, having already memorized them.

Katie sighed and put it away. *Why dream up obstacles now?* As Mam used to say, life was difficult enough without anticipating problems. Katie smiled, although her heart was sore. In her head, she could hear her mother's lilting Irish accent as she told her, "Patience, Katie darling. If something is for you, it won't go by you."

CHAPTER 7

"Thank God today is over. My poor old feet thought they were never going to stand still."

"Sit down, Nellie. Would you like some tea and some cake?" Katie said, looking with concern at the older woman's feet. Her ankles were swollen. She really should see a doctor.

"Just a drink, Katie girl. I don't think me getting any bigger is going to help my feet." Nellie laughed as she swatted her stomach. Her laugh faded as she caught the thoughtful expression on Katie's face. "What's wrong, love?"

"Nellie, do you know of a Mrs. Gantley from Boutwell Avenue?"

"Maura Gantley? Why are you asking? She hasn't

offered you a new position as a maid, has she? Don't know what I would do without you, Katie girl!"

Guilt making her stomach churn, Katie sought to reassure her friend.

"No, I haven't found a new job." The guilt got worse at the look of relief on Nellie's face. Katie put her hand in her pocket and pulled out the ad. "Read this. You won't like it, but please just read it through."

Nellie took the piece of paper, giving Katie a searching glance before putting on her spectacles and reading the ad slowly. Katie saw how the cook was using her fingers to move from word to word. *I should have read it out to her.* She kept forgetting that not everyone had the benefit of a Mam who had insisted all her children, boys and girls, were taught their letters.

Nellie finished the piece, removed her glasses and stared at Katie for a few seconds. The silence grew uncomfortable.

"You think I am wanton for even considering marrying a man I haven't met, don't you?"

"Not wanton, Katie girl, but desperate. I know you are unhappy here, but to go to this length to get away? Surely there are other alternatives?"

Katie shook her head. "You and I know there isn't much choice for the likes of us. I don't want to leave you, Nellie. You've been like a mother to Ellen and myself, but I can't stand living here for much longer. Every time Aunt Margaret makes a spiteful remark about our Liam, I am set to slap her."

"Liam? Oh, he's the one who…" Nellie stopped, her embarrassment obvious.

"Yes, he's the one who got arrested and the reason Daddy lost his farm. Liam didn't do anything. He wasn't involved with the gang who robbed and set fire to the big house but the English soldiers didn't believe him. He was an Irish lad, and in their eyes, that made him guilty. He didn't help himself either. He could have told them who really did it."

"The mistress should believe you. He's her kin, too. She is a funny woman. She used to be—well, not nice, exactly, but more pleasant. But the loss of the babies and what with your uncle…" Nellie's face grew redder. "Anyway, enough of that talk. Let's go back to the matter at hand. Maura Gantley is a respectable woman who has lived in Boutwell Avenue for more years than I care to remember. She has, or at least had, four boys of her own. One died from smallpox and I think one went to Europe. Maybe to England. The other two went west. Maybe that's what started this service of hers?" Nellie picked up the ad again. "Imagine marrying a man you haven't even laid eyes on. Could you do that, Katie girl?"

"I think I have to, Nellie. I have to think of Ellen.

She can't live here on her own, and she is too young and naïve to go into service. It's not that I don't trust her. She works hard, but you know what she is like. Her head is in the clouds most of the time. She shouldn't be working this hard either. Her health isn't up to it."

"What would your Mam, God rest her soul, think about you marrying a man like this? Surely she would have planned something different."

"It was all supposed to be different." Katie couldn't keep the bitterness from her voice. "But being poor in Ireland isn't any different to being poor in America. You don't have any rights. If someone rich accuses you of doing something, it doesn't matter if you are innocent. You and your whole family pay the consequences. I was lucky. I'm still alive. Mam isn't."

The tears rolled down Katie's cheeks despite her best efforts to stop them. She clenched her hands over and over, trying her best to stop the flood, but it didn't work.

"Let them out, Katie girl. You need to grieve sometime. You spend all hours working and watching out for Ellen. You have got to feel the hurt and let it go. God will look after you. You are a good girl."

"God didn't look after my family, did He, Nellie? Why? They were good people. Liam had a girl waiting for him. They were going to be married. Mam was all excited about the wedding. He'd have been married over a year by now; Mam should have been bouncing a new grandbaby on her lap. Instead, she is dead, he's as good as dead and I don't know what happened to Siobhan."

"Kathleen O'Callaghan, you wash your mouth out now, you hear? God has his ways and it is not for us to reason why bad things happen." Nellie softened her tone, taking one of Katie's hands in hers. "Katie girl, you have to believe in God. What else makes life worthwhile? Say your prayers. Ask your Mam for help. I will pray, too. I will ask Him to relieve your sorrows, but also to pick a good man for you. I will help you get out of here, Katie girl. I will make sure of it, just as sure as my name is Nellie Power."

Katie crossed her fingers. "I promise to try praying more, Nellie. I have to go to church anyway, as I need a reference from Father Molloy. I don't know who else to ask."

"Your Aunt Margaret will write you a reference," Nellie said, a sparkle in her eyes. At Katie's questioning look, she continued. "Well, she won't know she wrote it. I know it's dishonest, but we must do what needs to be done. I will confess my sins, but not until you are on your way out West. Now what you doing still sitting here? You got a letter to write."

"Oh, I wish I could take you with me, Nellie. I

really do. Thank you." Katie gave the older woman a hug before racing toward the door. She heard Nellie mutter, "I love you, Katie girl, but I'm not going anywhere near Indian country. Not for you or nobody."

CHAPTER 8

Calm down. You won't impress Mrs. Gantley if you stand here shaking like a leaf. Katie counted backward from ten, trying to slow her breathing right down. She wanted to make a favorable impression, having determined going west was the best escape for her and Ellen.

She knocked and stood back as the butler opened the door. His face remained impassive when she asked to speak to Mrs. Gantley. Katie wondered how many other prospective brides he had shown into the lady's reception room. He motioned for Katie to follow him and led her into a parlor.

"Please take a seat. The mistress will be with you shortly." He turned and went out the door, leaving Katie alone.

The room smelled of beeswax and lavender. Katie

glanced around, her gaze taking in the walnut coffee table and small writing desk, the baby grand piano in the corner and the large overmantel. Although pale sunlight trickled through the window, she was glad of the small fire crackling in the grate.

Tempted as she was to stand in front of the heat to warm up her hands and feet, Katie perched at the edge of the sofa. She was afraid to sit back in case she got the beautiful cream slipcovers dirty. She held her hands in her lap in an effort to stop them shaking. *Get a hold of yourself.*

As the minutes ticked by, she gave in to temptation and leaned back into the comfortable couch. Her head rested against the tapestry coverings. She closed her eyes, daydreaming she was the lady of a house as fine as this one. Smiling, she imagined what her husband would look like. She was so caught up in her daydream that she didn't hear any footsteps in the hall outside. The noise of the door opening brought her back to earth with a start.

"Good afternoon."

Katie tried to stand, but her legs wouldn't follow her brain's instruction. She was mesmerized, looking at the woman who flowed rather than walked into the room. She was so elegant, Katie found herself to be tongue-tied despite the friendly face and soft smile looking back at her.

"Please don't get up. I am sorry to keep you waiting. I am afraid the rather unfortunate smell is the cookies I planned on serving."

Katie nodded. *Speak, for goodness sake. She is going to think you are simple minded.*

"Please excuse me, Mrs. Gantley. My name is Katie, I mean Kathleen O'Callaghan. I am in awe of your beautiful house."

Mrs. Gantley looked around the room as if seeing it for the first time. "It is rather pretty, isn't it? My husband and son travel abroad regularly. I am afraid they spoil me by bringing back unusual presents they feel I will enjoy. I love being surrounded by beautiful things. The world today can be rather ugly, don't you think, Miss O'Callaghan?"

Katie nodded but couldn't really imagine what ugliness Mrs. Gantley would have experienced.

A maid interrupted them, bringing coffee. The rich aroma made Katie's mouth water. She went to pick up a cup, but her hand shook so much she opted to wait for a few minutes. *I should have taken off my gloves when I first sat down. She will think I have no manners.*

"So why do you want to go out West, Miss O'Callaghan? Haven't you traveled far enough?" At Katie's surprised look, her host smiled before adding, "Your Irish accent is too strong for you to have been reared in Boston."

"Yes, ma'am. I mean, no, ma'am. Oh, I don't really know what I mean." If Katie had known any curse words, she would have used one silently now. She was making a fool of herself. Her host's eyes twinkled with laughter, which didn't help to ease Katie's embarrassment.

"Katie—you don't mind if I call you that do you?" Katie shook her head. "Good, I believe it suits you. Please try to relax. This meeting isn't a test. There are no right or wrong answers. I want every girl I meet to be sure she is doing the right thing for her circumstances. I am not in the business of sending women out West who would sooner head back home to their own beautiful countries."

Katie looked down at the luxurious carpet her feet had sunk into. *How honest did the woman want her to be?*

"No fear of that happening with me, ma'am. There is no home for me in Ireland. Not anymore." Katie sat up straighter in the chair. "I want to go out west, ma'am. I want to build a new home for me and my—well, that is to say, any children God may see fit to provide me with." Katie's cheeks reddened further and she had to resist the urge to use her gloved hands to cover them.

"Why out west? Why not stay here in Boston? I assume you came over to family?"

Katie nodded. "My Uncle Joseph and his wife

provide us—I mean me—with a home." Katie corrected herself quickly and hoped Mrs. Gantley hadn't noticed the slip. Now was not the time to mention she intended taking Ellen with her.

"I gather from your expression the living arrangements are not favorable."

"No, ma'am. It isn't that I am afraid of hard work or anything, but I want to be in charge of my own life. Not be a servant for anybody else, not even a member of my family."

"That's a sentiment I understand, but you know that in the eyes of the law your husband would be your master, don't you?"

"Well, yes, Ma'am, but at least I would be mistress of my own home. I am a good cook. Not great, but I am learning how to prepare American food such as flapjacks. I have a lot of experience as a housekeeper and can make a floor shine so good you could see your face in it." Katie stopped, hoping she didn't sound like she was boasting. The look Mrs. Gantley gave her suggested she was pleased with what she was hearing. Katie smiled slightly before saying, "I would hope my husband was a kind man and together we would form a happy home. One where everyone was treated well."

"What else would you like from the marriage?" asked Mrs. Gantley gently.

Katie looked down at her gloved hands. "I would

like to have children. At least two, but more if possible. Back home, there were always children running around, and I miss it." Katie pinched her wrist in an effort to distract her thoughts. She didn't want to dwell on thoughts of what home had been like. That would only lead to tears.

Taking a deep breath, she leaned forward in her seat. "I would also like my husband to be able to provide for us." At Mrs. Gantley's raised eyebrows, Katie swallowed hard before continuing. "I don't mean I want a rich man, but I am done with being dirt poor. If possible, I would like to marry someone with prospects. I will work hard, day and night, but I can only do that if there is some hope that my work will mean we have a secure future. Being financially secure is important."

To her surprise, Mrs. Gantley rose and walked around her desk to put a hand on Katie's shoulder.

"You are a very brave girl, Katie O'Callaghan. It took real courage to make a speech like that. I totally agree with your sentiments, which is why I make it a condition of any arrangement my girls enter into that their husband provide them with a home, at the very least. I have been responsible for arranging about forty matches since I started doing this five years ago. I am happy to say that thirty-eight of those have turned out well. The other two—well, I guess the less said about those the better."

Katie was dying to ask what happened in the other two cases, but her nerve failed at the closed expression on Mrs. Gantley's face.

"What happens now?" asked Katie after a few minutes of silence.

"I was just thinking about the three letters I have. I suggest you consider Mr. Cassidy. He mentions he has a ranch." At Katie's confused expression, Mrs. Gantley smiled and explained, "Think of it as a large farm. He will own horses and some cattle. There may be other animals as well, such as chickens, pigs, etc. At least you should never be hungry."

Katie smiled, but couldn't help wondering why, if he was wealthy, he needed a mail order bride. As if guessing her thoughts, Mrs. Gantley continued. "Men outnumber the women out west by about twenty to one. In some areas, that figure could be as high as fifty to one. You may have seen some cartoons in the paper suggesting that women are worth their weight in gold."

Katie shook her head. She hadn't had time to read newspapers but didn't think her uncle would have cartoons in his reading material.

"The lack of *decent* women explains why even relatively well-off men have to send East for their brides.

Of course, here in Boston, we appear to have the opposite problem. Quite a few women and not enough prospective husbands. Both my sons had to come home to find wives. That's part of the reason why I set up Boston Brides. My husband would say the real reason is that I am an incurable romantic."

Katie returned the woman's warm smile, her heart filling with hope for the first time since she had left Ireland. This was her chance. She was sure of it. She watched Mrs. Gantley rustle through some papers on her desk before she found something and handed it over to Katie.

Before she took it, Katie cleared her throat.

"Mrs. Gantley, you haven't said how much you charge for providing this service. I wouldn't want to waste your time."

"Oh, don't worry about that, dear. The men pay a small fee for my services. They also provide you with a train ticket and some offer to cover additional expenses you may incur, such as a wedding dress, etc."

I could have done with knowing that a few days ago. It would have saved me a few nights of lost sleep. If Mr. Cassidy covers my train fare and the Boston Brides fee, I should have enough in savings to pay for Ellen's ticket.

Katie smiled broadly as she took the letter. *Imagine, my future husband wrote this.*

All romantic notions she had entertained died as

soon as she read the contents. It sounded as interesting as her shopping list for the store. Confused and more than slightly disappointed, she raised her head to find Mrs. Gantley looking at her with a gentle expression on her face.

"Remember, my dear, that these men are not schooled in the ways of courtship. You cannot expect them to act in a similar manner to those you read about in your romance books. They need some help to round off their rough edges. Some may need more assistance than others."

Feeling ashamed for letting her romantic notions overtake the practical side, she came to a swift decision. "You are absolutely correct. I will take Mr. Cassidy if he finds me agreeable. What should I do now?"

"I would like you to think on it for a few days. There is no real rush." Mrs. Gantley held her head to one side as if asking a question.

Katie ignored the curiosity in her eyes. She wanted to move as fast as possible, but that may make Mrs. Gantley suspicious. Fighting her desire to proceed immediately, she took a deep breath before saying. "Thank you. I feel certain I would like to proceed, but perhaps a day or two to think about it would be a good idea."

Mrs. Gantley nodded in agreement. "Can you

come back to see me in a few days? We can then write back to Mr. Cassidy, assuming you haven't had a change of heart."

Please don't talk about changing my mind. I don't want to start wondering if there is any other way. There isn't and that's all there is to it. She couldn't live with the stress of living under Margaret's roof for much longer and it wasn't good for Ellen, either. This was the best decision for both of them.

Katie stood, willing her body not to shake. She extended her hand.

"Thank you very much, Mrs. Gantley. I will call back to see you next Wednesday. I won't be able to get out of the house before then other than for services on Sunday."

"Maybe by then my new cook will have gotten used to the oven and we can have cookies with our coffee." Mrs. Gantley laughed, the sound reminding Katie of tinkling bells.

If only it was just burnt cookies I had to worry about.

CHAPTER 9

"You are a good girl, you know. Pretty as a picture, too," Nellie gave Katie a grateful look as she sat down. Their day had started at 6am and it was coming up on 11pm.

Katie was concerned. Nellie's breathing was faster than usual. She didn't know how old the cook was, but she must be at least fifty.

"Nellie, I think I should call a doctor."

Nellie stood but a wave of dizziness made her sit back down. "I'll be okay in a minute or two. I just been working a mite too hard lately."

"That's not it and you know it. You' been having trouble breathing for weeks now. You need to rest. Do you not have somewhere else to go? Could you not go live with your sister?"

"She's asked me, but I don't know if I could live

with her. Two women in the same kitchen don't work too good, in my experience. And anyways, if I left, you two would be all alone. You know she won't hire a new cook if she knows you can make stuff as well as I do."

"Nonsense, Nellie. Nobody can cook as well as you do. Never mind about us. We won't be staying."

Nellie sat up straighter. "You got something to tell me, Kathleen O'Callaghan?'

Katie gulped. She tried to speak but couldn't find her voice, so she nodded.

"You need to try harder than that, my girl. Has Mrs. Gantley found you a husband?"

Katie nodded again, but stared at the floor, her fingers opening and closing as the reality of what she had decided to do hit home. She was going to marry Mr. Cassidy and move out west. Just as soon as it could be arranged.

"Sit down, girl, and tell me." Nellie patted the chair nearest to her.

"Mrs. Gantley showed me a letter from a gentleman. He's got a farm—I mean a ranch—in Colorado near a town called Clear Creek. He needs a wife. He will pay all my expenses. Oh, Nellie, tell me I am doing the right thing."

Nellie looked at her sadly, her eyes filling with tears.

Don't cry, please don't cry. Katie took a deep breath to try to get her own emotions under control.

"It's my only chance, Nellie. You know there is nowhere for me to go in Boston. Not with Ellen to look after. I couldn't bear for her to live in the orphanage or be adopted by strangers."

"What about you, darling girl? Are you ready to marry this Mr. Cassidy? A stranger?"

"Yes. I am. I have to tell Mrs. Gantley tomorrow. She showed me his letter and she has checked his references. He seems quite nice." Katie crossed her fingers at the lie. Nice was hardly the term that could be attached to the single-paged note he had sent, but Nellie didn't need to know that.

She decided to change the subject. "Nellie, you need to think about yourself for once. You're not getting any younger. Go live with your sister. I can't leave knowing Aunt Margaret may blame you."

"I'll think it over," Nellie said, stirring her coffee. She looked over at Katie. "I pray every night you get the life you deserve, my darling girl. Mr. Cassidy may be your Prince Charming."

"I certainly hope so, Nellie. It can't be worse than staying here." They both heard steps coming toward the kitchen. "That will be Ellen back with more dishes. I haven't told her yet."

* * *

THE NEXT MORNING, stomach churning, Katie dressed carefully. Closing the door of her uncle's house behind her, she couldn't resist smiling. It wouldn't be long now before she could leave for good. Her smile faltered. She might be over eighteen, but her uncle was still Ellen's guardian. He could stop them leaving. *Let him try. She would sneak Ellen out of the house. No way was she leaving her sister behind.*

Pushing the negative thoughts to the back of her mind, she walked quickly, arriving at Mrs. Gantley's house slightly breathless. The butler answered and showed her into the parlor. Mrs. Gantley looked up and smiled warmly.

"Katie, how nice to see you again. I take it from your happy face that you haven't changed your mind about Mr. Cassidy."

"No, ma'am. I want to be a mail order bride, the sooner the better."

Mrs. Gantley's smile reached her eyes. "I see you haven't gained any patience. Take a seat, my dear, and we will get the paperwork sorted. But first, let me ring for some coffee. I think we should skip the cookies. They haven't improved since last time."

Katie sat and waited for Mrs. Gantley to explain what would happen next.

"We will both write to Mr. Cassidy. You should tell him a little about yourself, your age and what you are looking for. I will write a letter of introduction and enclose your references. I can post the letters tomorrow and we should have an answer back within about a month."

At Katie's nod, Mrs. Gantley took some writing materials from her desk. Together, they worked in silence. Katie tried her best to describe herself objectively. She found herself using words like strong, reliable and dependable. *I sound like a horse.* When he gets this letter, Mr. Cassidy will run a mile in the opposite direction. She handed the letter to Mrs. Gantley, who laughed loudly when she read Katie's first attempt.

"Sorry to laugh at you, dear, but perhaps you could add that you are rather striking, with glorious black hair and beautiful violet eyes. You have very unusual coloring, especially for an Irish girl. People always expect red hair and freckles."

Katie, although pleased, looked down at the floor. "I couldn't say things like that, Mrs. Gantley. It wouldn't be proper."

"Well now, I wish I could be there when the train arrives and Mr. Cassidy first lays eyes on you. He will be struck dumb."

Katie allowed herself to bask in the warmth of the praise before telling herself off. *All that matters is he marries me and I can look after Ellen and myself. I cannot afford to indulge in romantic notions.*

"Do you have any questions? You haven't asked about his religious background. Being Irish, I assume you are Catholic. Do you not wish to marry into the same faith?"

Katie shook her head. Being Catholic was no guarantee of a man's good nature. Uncle Joseph was proof of that. "I would prefer a good Christian man to one who follows a faith just for appearance's sake. He says in his letter he is an upstanding citizen and he enclosed a reference from his minister. That's enough for now."

"Well, if you are sure, I will post these letters in the morning." Mrs. Gantley looked at Katie, seeking confirmation.

"Yes, ma'am. Thank you for everything. I must go now, but I will call to see you in a month. You know where to reach me if you have an answer before then."

Mrs. Gantley chuckled and rose to her feet. Taking Katie's arm, she escorted her to the front door. "You are a charming young woman. Mr. Cassidy will be a lucky man."

"Thank you, Mrs. Gantley." *I hope he still feels lucky when he realizes he is taking on his bride's young sister.* Katie tied the ribbons of her bonnet under her chin. Before she left, she turned to the other woman. "Mrs.

Gantley, you wouldn't perhaps be in the market for a new cook? I know a lady who makes wonderful cookies."

"Not at the moment, dear. I promised Ida's father I would look out for her. I live in hope she will improve. I pray nightly for a miracle." Mrs. Gantley smiled to take the sting out of the words.

She really is a kind lady. Nellie would be lucky to have her as a mistress. She's not a bit like Aunt Margaret. Katie realized Mrs. Gantley was speaking to her.

"Would your friend be interested in becoming a mail order bride? Almost every man who writes to me wants a wife who can cook."

Katie burst out laughing at the thought of Nellie heading west to marry anyone. She shook her head. "Nellie, the cook where I currently live, thinks five miles outside Boston is the Wild West." Katie shook the other woman's hand. "See you in a month, Mrs. Gantley, and thank you."

Katie left the house still smiling at the thought of Nellie heading west. She almost skipped down the street but restrained herself. She was going to be married and mature ladies didn't behave like silly young girls.

CHAPTER 10

CLEAR CREEK

Montis stomped across the street, his spurs sending the dust flying, away from the post office and toward the saloon. He needed a drink. Now. Barging in, he went up to the bar. He tossed back the whiskey before demanding another from the barkeep.

He hadn't expected to find a letter waiting for him when he got to town. It had been so long since Virgil had sent his note about a bride, Montis had almost forgotten he had agreed to get hitched. Now it turned out his darn brother had been intercepting *his* letters and corresponding with Boston Brides on his behalf. He thumped the bar, despite the look the barkeep sent him. If he hadn't come into town today, he wouldn't even know the gal was on her way.

He looked at the letter again. Seems Virgil had sent

them the money for the ticket plus extras. The note was so thankful for his generosity. He snorted. Virgil must have been more desperate than he realized if he had sent more money than was required.

He was so caught up, he didn't notice the saloon girl sidle up to him.

"You look thirsty," she said, her eyes gliding over him.

"Leave me be."

"I was just trying to be friendly." She stalked off.

Montis didn't want anyone being friendly, least of all a woman. He had enough troubles in that department. The letter in his pocket was the reason he was drinking whiskey like someone caught in the desert with a dry canteen.

Women. He didn't need that kind of trouble. *Well, you got it now, you best get on with it.*

He took the letter out of his pocket again. At least she sounded pretty. Maybe even beautiful. A girl who looked good couldn't be like his ma. Could she? He'd find out soon enough. According to the letter, she would arrive in about two weeks. He was glad Virgil was on one of his trips. He didn't need his brother around, messing up his plans. If he was here, he would insist he marry the girl as soon as she got off the train. But this way, he could wait a couple of days and see what she was really like. If she was anything like his ma, she could go right back to Boston. If Virgil didn't like that, then he could marry her.

Feeling clever, he looked around for the saloon girl. Hell, he wasn't married yet. Some company might be nice. He smiled at the saloon girl, who looked warily at him, before realizing he was grinning at her. Returning his smile, but without losing the wary look in her eyes, she sashayed back over to him.

"Feeling better?"

"Much. I'd like to take you up on that offer of a drink. Have one yourself, too." He nodded at the chair beside him as she called the barkeep over. He didn't bat an eye when she asked for a bottle and two glasses. He had money in his pocket, a pretty girl on his arm and his marriage woes sorted. What more could he ask for? He was a lucky man, indeed.

CHAPTER 11

BOSTON

Mrs. Gantley had sent Katie a note asking her to call. Once more, Nellie came to her rescue, sending Katie out on an errand. Katie ran almost the whole way to Mrs. Gantley's house. The butler looked as if he was trying not to smile at her flushed cheeks and breathlessness. He showed her into the same room as before where Mrs. Gantley was seated reading a book.

"Good news, Katie. Mr. Cassidy sent me a letter enclosing your train ticket and also some money for your needs. He has been more than generous. I hope you will write to me and let me know how you get on."

Katie nodded, not trusting herself to speak. She was so excited, she was sure the words would come out in a high squeak.

"You will travel a week from today. Does that sound good to you?"

"Yes, Mrs. Gantley. Thank you for everything."

"It's a pleasure, dear. I hope you and Mr. Cassidy have years of happiness ahead of you."

Katie hoped so, too. God had answered all her prayers. *Nellie. She was leaving her alone.*

"Katie, you probably noticed I didn't offer you cookies today. I am pleased to say Ida has decided to leave us and become a mail order bride. Her betrothed is a chef, so her lack of cooking skills isn't an issue, thank goodness."

Katie smiled at the joke. She was happy to hear more proof Mrs. Gantley made an effort to make almost perfect matches.

"You mentioned last time you knew of a good cook. I was wondering if she would be still available. My beloved husband is getting rather cranky for want of a decent home-cooked meal."

Katie was nodding even before Mrs. Gantley had finished her sentence. "Yes, Ma'am. Nellie, my friend, is a great cook and she wants to stay in Boston. She is looking for a position in a smaller establishment." Katie didn't want to say Nellie worked for her aunt. "Her current employers entertain a lot."

"Wonderful. Would she come and see me? Do tell her to hurry, will you, please, Katie? And remember to write to me and let me know how you are. I am looking forward to counting your match as another success."

"Yes, Mrs. Gantley, and thank you for everything."

Katie almost flew home. She couldn't believe her good luck. Not only did she have sufficient money to cover Ellen's train fare, but she had a bit left over to buy some essentials for their long trip. Nellie had a new position with a mistress who would treat her fairly. Life was wonderful. Katie thought she would burst with happiness.

She considered running to the orphanage to tell Mary Ryan about her good fortune, but it was too late. She would see her on Sunday. Maybe Mary would decide to become a mail order bride, too.

It was only when she reached her aunt's house that Katie realized she had forgotten something. *How will I get Ellen out of the house without Uncle Joseph stopping us? Nellie will help.*

* * *

KATIE AND ELLEN sat waiting in the priest's sitting room.

Mary and Catherine were late. Katie played with her fingers. They had to come tonight.

"We can't go without saying goodbye to the girls,"

Ellen said.

"Shhh, Ellen. Mrs. Raines might hear you."

"Why does it have to be a secret?" Ellen pouted.

"You know why. Uncle Joseph could stop you coming with me. I don't want to take that risk."

The door opened just then. Mary and Catherine came into the room looking sadder than ever.

"What's up with you two?" Ellen asked.

"A couple has enquired about adopting Catherine. Mother Superior said it would be a great opportunity. The people have money and will be able to send her to a nice school. She will live in a big house, have plenty to eat and lots of nice clothes." Mary stopped talking, her face pale as she took a seat. Catherine threw herself at her sister.

"I'm not going. I won't leave you, Mary. You can't make me go."

Mary put her arms around her younger sister, trying to stop her crying.

"I can't stop them, Cathy, you know that."

"We can ask Father Molloy if he can do something. Maybe the people don't know you are sisters. They might take the two of you?" Katie said, despite knowing most couples didn't adopt a seventeen-year-old.

"That's a great idea. We will speak to Father Molloy later, Cathy. Now why don't you and Ellen go to the kitchen and ask Mrs. Raines if she would like some help. I need to speak to Katie."

Katie and Mary sat on the sofa, whispering.

"Mother Superior says she already told them Catherine had an older sister, but they are not interested. It's a fantastic opportunity for her. I love her too much to stand in her way."

"Oh, Mary, I wish I knew what to say to you. I couldn't bear if anyone were to try to take Ellen away from me. That's why I have to go away."

Mary sat upright. "Where? Can we go, too?"

Katie shook her head. "Not this time, but you may be able to follow us. I am getting married."

"Married?" Mary's eyes grew wide with shock. "I didn't even know you had been courting."

"I haven't. I am going to be a mail order bride." At the confused look on her friend's face, Katie continued. "I met a lady called Mrs. Gantley. She arranges weddings between girls from the East and men of the West. There is a lack of women out west, so men need to send away for brides. I have written to Mr. Cassidy and we have agreed to wed. We leave for the Colorado Territory on Wednesday. I will write to you as soon as I can. Maybe Mr. Cassidy will have a friend who needs a wife and you can come out, too?"

Mary stayed silent.

"Don't be judging me, Mary Ryan. This is the only

way I can be sure that myself and Ellen stay together. I have to get away from Boston."

"Does Mr. Cassidy not mind Ellen coming?" Katie avoided Mary's gaze. "Oh, Katie, you didn't tell him did you?" Katie shook her head. "What if he sends Ellen back?"

"He won't," Katie said firmly, crossing her fingers.

"Married? I don't believe it. It hardly seems like yesterday when we were getting on the boat in Galway."

"Don't, Mary. Leave the past behind us. It's too painful to think about that now. We can only look to the future. Please give me your blessing."

Mary threw her arms around Katie, holding her close as she cried her eyes out. "You are my dearest friend, Katie O'Callaghan and I will pray every night that you find happiness in Colorado. Don't forget to write to us. You are so brave. I wish I had half your strength."

"You do, Mary. Pray to your Mam to help you to stay together. Speak to Mrs. Gantley, too. She told me she had lots of men looking for wives."

"I couldn't go somewhere I knew nobody. I will wait for you to write to me. You can find me a husband near to where you live and then we can all be together again. Maybe even happy."

"Who's not happy?" Father Molloy said as he

walked into the room accompanied by the two younger girls. "Are Mrs. Raines's cakes not up to their usual standard?"

"They are lovely, Father. Ellen and I have to leave now. Uncle Joseph expects us back early tonight. Mary has want of a quiet word with you." Katie wanted to thank the priest for everything he had done for them, but she couldn't risk him becoming suspicious. Nothing could jeopardize her plans. Not at this stage. "Goodnight, Father, and thank you. Goodbye, girls." Katie hurried out the door before her tears started falling.

* * *

Denver Colorado

Daniel Sullivan kicked at the boardwalk. Trust the train to be late today of all days. He needed to get home to Clover Springs. The fancy clothes he was wearing were making him itch all over.

He scowled, frustration and the resulting lack of sleep making him uncharacteristically bad tempered. *Why did I even bother coming here? I should have known better than to believe I could buy the store.* He'd allowed himself to dream of a new life away from the trail.

Ranching wasn't for him. It suited his brother Davy and the ranch had prospered since Ma had handed over the reins. Daniel wanted something different. He had considered opening a general store but immediately dismissed the idea as he would be in competition with Brook's mercantile. But then Mr. Brook decided it was time to head back East to his daughter and her family. He wasn't getting any younger, and now that Clover Springs had a railroad, his store could be sold for a nice profit.

Daniel's grandfather and Mr. Brook had met on the wagon train that brought them to Clover Springs all those years ago. Legend had it that Grandpa Sullivan had taken the young Mr. Brook under his wing; hence the offer to sell Daniel the store at a good price. Although he had sufficient savings to meet the down payment, he needed a loan to buy the store.

His scowl deepened as he went over the meeting with Mr. Winkle, the insufferable banker he had met the day before. He had turned up for the meeting at the Denver bank dressed in his best clothes. His collar chafed his neck and his knees had shaken. He hated being in the city. All those buildings and people made him feel as if he couldn't breathe. It hadn't helped when the bank clerk had kept him waiting for well over an hour. As if to prove he was somehow more important a human being just because he worked in a bank.

Mr. Winkle had been as officious as one would expect from a banker. He had read every word, every letter and figure regarding the accounts Mr. Brook had provided. It was obvious the store was turning a healthy profit and the price was reasonable.

"How did you acquire your savings, Mr. Sullivan?"

"When my pa died, he left me a little money. I bought some steers from the local ranch boss. I worked for him as a wrangler for a couple of years. I saved what I could."

"So, you have never actually worked in a store?"

"No, sir, but I know how to do figures and keep books. Mr. Brook, the current owner, will stay to train me for a month to six weeks. He will head back East when the summer comes."

"You believe you can learn how to manage a business in a couple of months?"

Daniel didn't appreciate the banker's tone.

"Yes. The store is well placed with regular customers in a growing town. How hard can it be?" Daniel smiled, hoping to convince the banker he was in earnest.

"Perhaps, Mr. Sullivan, but what happens when the

call to go west comes again? I know what you cowboys are like. You try to settle down, but the wanderlust …"

"Now listen here. I am no dumb cowboy. I ran those cattle to make sufficient money to buy me a business and settle down. I don't know how many days you have spent on the trail, but believe me, I have no hankering for that life. Not anymore. Now are you going to lend me the money or should I take my business elsewhere?" Daniel tried to get a hold on his temper. They both knew there wasn't really anywhere else for him to get the funds he needed.

Mr. Winkle surveyed the papers and Daniel for a few minutes. Just as he felt the silence would go on forever, Daniel was surprised to see a ghost of a smile flicker across the banker's face.

"Okay, Mr. Sullivan. You have your loan."

"Thank you kindly, sir. I won't let you down. I apologize for being ornery." Daniel rose to shake the banker's hand.

"Not so fast, son. In addition to the mortgage on the property, the bank will have one further condition." The banker stared straight at Daniel. "You must be married by the time you close the sale."

"Married?" Daniel sat with a bump. "In less than a month? But who? Why? Where am I supposed to find a bride?"

"We are a bank, not a marriage bureau, so I am afraid I cannot help you answer the who or where." The banker smiled as if to convey it was a joke. At Daniel's blank stare, he continued swiftly. "But the why is simple. As a married man, you are less likely to answer the call of the trail. Now, do you want this loan or not?"

The sound of the train's whistle interrupted his musings. Daniel stood back to give the passengers leaving the train some room. Ma would be delighted he had to get married. She hated him being on the trail. She wanted her sons close and preferably married with children. Daniel laughed. Maybe his Ma had been in cahoots with Mr. Winkle all along. He wouldn't put anything past her.

He stepped into the train car, his bad mood all but disappearing. He would soon be home, back in his normal clothes eating Ma's cooking. He would buy the store. He wasn't going to let Mr. Winkle stand in his way. There had to be at least one eligible woman in Clover Springs. Ma had mentioned something about a widow who did some washing. He didn't know anything about her, other than her husband's sudden death had left her badly off. She could be ancient, ugly or both but given her being a widow, she wouldn't be looking for a love match. It could be a business arrangement. The banker hadn't said he had to stay married forever, just at the time the loan was drawn.

Satisfied he had found the answer to his problems, he took his seat pulling his hat down over his eyes. In no time at all, he was fast asleep.

CHAPTER 12

Katie sat on the train seat, cuddling Ellen. With each passing hour, Boston and their horrible relations were left further behind. She couldn't believe their plan had worked. Uncle Joseph had gone out of town and Nellie had somehow convinced Aunt Margaret to go to bed and rest. The girls had been able to sneak out of the house. Katie had written to Father Molloy, telling him the whole story and explaining why she was leaving. She hadn't told him where they were going, as she couldn't risk the priest telling Uncle Joseph—although she did wish she could be present when the priest confronted Uncle Joseph about his treatment of the Ryan girls. She didn't think the old man would understand how anyone could have left the girls to fend for themselves.

Aunt Margaret would get her comeuppance when

she realized Nellie was leaving, too. Mrs. Gantley had welcomed Nellie like a long lost relative. Katie was glad her friend was going to a house where she would be treated properly. Nellie had promised to keep an eye on Mary Ryan. She had wondered if Mrs. Gantley might take on the girl to help in the house. Katie didn't know if that would happen, but she kept her fingers crossed. *Mam, work your magic and look after the Ryan girls as well as Nellie, please.*

Katie looked out the train window, her thoughts of Mam bringing tears. If Mam were still alive, she wouldn't be going half way across the country to marry a man she hadn't met. She wouldn't be dragging Ellen with her either.

She hadn't told Mr. Cassidy about Ellen. She shook her head in frustration. It was too late for regrets. She had signed a contract. There was no going back now. Clear Creek, Colorado. That was her new home.

Mam always said every cloud had a silver lining. Katie looked at the clear blue sky, not a cloud in sight. She sighed. She had to think positively. She and Ellen were together and in good health. *Yes, but for how long?* Nellie had told them awful stories about life on the frontier. Indians, blizzards and creepy critters bigger than the size of your hand. *Stop it.* What other good things could she think of?

There was no Lord Harrington in Clear Creek.

Katie's hands clenched, her knuckles whitening, as she thought of the man who had evicted Katie and her family along with sixty other families in their village. Katie's tears threatened to overflow as the memory of her father's face filled her mind. She knew it had taken every ounce of strength he possessed not to raise a hand to the soldiers who had come to oversee the evictions. There was no point in arguing their case. It didn't matter that their rent payments were up to date or that they had spent the last four years working as a community to reclaim over four hundred acres from the surrounding bog lands and turned it into fine pasture.

Katie grimaced. Reclaiming that bog had been their undoing. Lord Harrington, or his despised land agent, had realized the value of grazing land and had decided to turn their village into one large pasture. They had arrested Liam and some of the other young men and sent them to prison in England . That wasn't enough. They wanted to destroy their village, and accusing the villagers of hiding rebels gave them that excuse.

Katie closed her eyes, trying not to relive the nightmare that had sent her to America. She saw the soldiers pull the roofs from their homes while the women of the village clung to the doorposts. Katie's father had tried to restrain his wife but at the last minute, she broke free of his hold and had run back into their home, wanting to save a family heirloom. The roof had groaned loudly before caving in just as she disappeared through the doorway. Soldiers and villagers alike had to stop her father from going in after his wife. There was nothing they could do for the poor lady now.

Katie blinked, trying to clear the gruesome images from her mind. She didn't want to think of her father and the family she had left behind in Galway. She must look to the future and look for that silver lining just as Mam had taught her. She looked up again at the sky. *Mam, if you are up there, please help me make this marriage work. I'm scared. What if he doesn't like me? Or what if he won't take Ellen and sends us back?*

She felt her sister squeeze her hand.

"You all right, Katie? Your face was all screwed up when you were sleeping."

"I am fine, sweetheart. I was dreaming of Horace. Do you remember how badly he smelled?"

Katie was relieved to see the worried frown on her younger sister's face replaced by the ghost of a smile.

"He sure smelt bad, but he tasted so good. If I close my eyes, I can still taste Mam's Christmas dinner. I know the youngsters were upset, but I wouldn't mind a piece of Horace now." Ellen unconsciously licked her lips. It had been a long time since they had eaten.

"Excuse me, Miss, but did you just say you ate a man called Horace?"

Katie and Ellen looked at the older man sitting across from them who was making no effort to hide his disdain. Katie didn't know if it was their clothes, their accents or the fact that they were traveling without a chaperone that he disagreed with most. She didn't care for him, either. He reminded her of Captain Brown, the officer in charge of the soldiers who had arrested Liam, and so heartlessly thrown them out of their home.

"Our conversation is of no concern to you, sir, but please put your mind at ease. We killed a pig. My younger brother named him Horace, as he said he looked like our landlord's son."

Katie turned to gaze out the window. She didn't want to look at Ellen, sure if she did, they would both dissolve into fits of giggles. Out of the corner of her eye, she spotted a younger male passenger holding his hand to his mouth as if to hide a smile. She was drawn to look at him and blushed scarlet when he caught her gaze and winked back at her. She knew she should look away but she couldn't. It was forward of him to behave like that, but instead of being angry, she was surprised to find her stomach doing somersaults. Her eyes moved over him. He was well dressed in a crisp white shirt and tailored suit. Self consciously she rubbed at the wrinkles in her clothes. After several weeks traveling, she must look a sight. She wondered where he was going? He looked like a business man – maybe a banker? Despite her best intentions, her gaze wandered back up to his eyes. Oh no. He had caught her. He raised an eyebrow, his eyes and lips twitching with barely suppressed laughter. She wondered what his laugh sounded like?

Kathleen O'Callaghan, you are betrothed to another. You cannot be making eyes at a stranger, even if he is gorgeous. Dragging her eyes away, she forced herself to look out the window.

CHAPTER 13

Daniel had nearly bitten through his tongue in an effort not to laugh loudly at the image the girls had just described but when her eyes met his, all thoughts of laughter left him. He was no innocent but he couldn't remember ever reacting to a woman as strongly as this. Her voice made the skin on his neck tingle. She was gorgeous despite her wrinkled and slightly grubby clothes. Her skin looked so soft. He had to sit on his hand, the temptation to touch her was so strong.

He couldn't believe he had missed her when he got into the train car. He wouldn't have fallen asleep!

He guessed she was traveling with her sister as there was some resemblance. They were both beautiful with black hair and slightly tanned skin. Although their accents were Irish, they looked Spanish. The younger girl had blue eyes but the older one had eyes the color of violets. He had been mesmerized as they flashed with anger at the older passenger.

She reminded him of his older sister, Elizabeth. She had a fiery temper, too, and didn't suffer fools gladly. She had married Daniel's best friend about five years back. She kept her husband Harry and their two young sons in line, but his friend wouldn't have it any other way.

Amused, he watched as she examined him, waiting for her eyes to return to his face. She blushed furiously, the glow on her cheeks making her even more attractive. He had to bite his tongue again as she swiveled to stare out the window. He wasn't the only one who felt the attraction between them.

He fidgeted in his seat trying to sit more comfortably. He wanted to stretch out his legs; difficult to do anyway in the confined space but impossible when one was over six feet tall.

He watched her as she gazed intently out the window. She sure seemed to find the endless grass prairie mighty interesting. Where was she going? Why was she traveling alone with a young girl? Didn't she know how dangerous this territory could be? Especially for a woman who looked like she did. Was she married? He glanced at her hands but she was wearing gloves. He decided she wasn't. No man in his right mind would let his wife travel unaccompanied. He definitely wouldn't. Daniel sat up straighter. Where had that thought come from? Until yesterday, getting married hadn't been on his agenda. His ambitions to build a bigger, more profitable store came first. Plenty of time for settling down when he was older. But if his wife looked like the dark haired stranger, maybe getting wed wasn't such a bad idea after all. For the first time, he wished Ma had accompanied him on the trip to Denver. She could have struck up a conversation with the young ladies. It wasn't proper for him to just start talking to her.

CHAPTER 14

The conductor wandered through the train car, checking on the occupants. He caught Katie staring at him and gave her a cheerful smile. He had a friendly face but looked rather old to be working. She could see him sitting in a rocking chair on one side of the fire, his wife sitting on the other side.

"How are you this fine day, ladies?"

Katie smiled at Ellen's reaction. The younger girl got a thrill out of being addressed like an adult.

"I'm hungry," Ellen said. "Do the settlers eat similar type food to what we have been eating in Boston, Mr. Smithson?"

"I don't know what you ate, young lady, but out here it depends on who's entertaining. Most of the settlers will hunt for game and meat to provide for their families. The womenfolk can make real tasty meals from bison or buffalo as well as guinea fowl and squirrels."

"You eat bison?" Ellen curled her lip in distaste.

"Yes, Miss, and mighty tasty they are, too. The womenfolk grow corn, tomatoes and mushrooms in their gardens as well as many different herbs. Peaches and apples allow for some fine desserts." Mr. Smithson patted his stomach. "My Annie makes a mighty fine peach cobbler."

Katie listened with half an ear as the conductor described all the different foods to Ellen. She hadn't heard of half the varieties of meat. *I only hope Mr. Cassidy has a cook who can train me.* She stared at the bison grazing on the prairie. She couldn't imagine any of those enormous animals landing in her cooking pot.

She gazed in awe at the snow-covered mountain-tops on the distant skyline. The view was incredible. She wondered what it would be like to climb to the top of one of these mountains. They seemed to be higher than the clouds, yet someone had mentioned there were many miners up there looking for the next big silver or gold deposits. It must be wonderful to be a man and have the freedom to climb mountains or go exploring the world, instead of having to marry a stranger in order to secure your future.

. . .

DANIEL WONDERED why the young woman looked so upset. He silently cursed polite conventions that prevented him from talking to her. She had been smiling as she looked at the view but now her face was full of sadness. He had heard of the troubles in Ireland. Many people were leaving to find new lives in America. Was she one of them? Was that why they were traveling alone? He wished Mr. Smithson, the conductor, would come back into the car. Mr. Smithson had stayed at Ma's boarding house before. He was a friendly and talkative man.

CHAPTER 15

At the sound of the first gunshot, Ellen screamed and dug her nails into Katie's arm. The engine came to a shuddering halt, throwing them both forward in their seats. They heard shouts to get off the train.

"Put your hands over your head. Nobody will get hurt if you do as you are told."

Katie took Ellen's shaking hand and stood up. Her eyes widened as she noticed the young man opposite take his gun out of his holster.

Before she could say anything, another passenger hissed, "Put that away, son. You heard them. They have no reason to hurt us. It's the gold they want, not us. These ladies don't want to get caught in any crossfire."

The younger man reluctantly put his gun back and

moved toward the door of the train car. He jumped down and stood with his hands over his head. Katie pulled Ellen clear of the seat, and, pushing her sister behind her, followed the younger man's lead. She climbed out. The young man went to offer her assistance, but a shout from the train robber told him to stand still. The robber turned to Katie.

"I told you to put your hands on your head."

"You try climbing out of a train carriage wearing a dress and holding your hands over your head," Katie shot back at the train robber. She turned and helped Ellen disembark. Holding hands, they moved slowly to the side to join the other passengers.

She watched as the other passengers exited their cars. They held their hands over their heads as one of the train robbers removed the men's guns. The raiders were wearing masks.

"Gold, jewels, cash into the bag now. Be quick, mind. We don't got all day."

The passengers handed over their valuables to one of the raiders as the other held a gun on them. Katie could see other masked men threatening the conductor. She didn't know what he said, but cried out as they shot him. Instinctively, she let Ellen's hand fall and moved forward to help, but found a hand at her side pulling her back. She looked into the face of the young man from their train car.

"Nothing you can do. Stand still," he whispered out of the side of his mouth.

Katie did as she was told.

The train robber who had shot the conductor kicked the body before heading over to where the passengers stood. He helped to relieve some of the men of their wallets.

"Got anything in there, pretty lady?" he sneered as he came closer. She recoiled, the stink from his rotten teeth causing her stomach to lurch.

"No, but you are welcome to check." She threw her reticule at his feet, ignoring Ellen's intake of breath.

"You're a feisty filly. Maybe I should take you with me and show you some manners." He leered at her.

Katie shivered with revulsion, trying to resist the urge to smack his face. Her gaze held his. She knew he was taunting her, as if he knew how hard it was for her not to retaliate. It was the day with the soldiers all over again. Having to stand by, helpless, powerless to prevent something awful from happening.

"Billy, come on. We got to get out of here. That conductor is dead. We will swing for this. You were only supposed to grab the gold."

Billy turned to the man who had shouted, and at the same time, the young man from her carriage pushed Katie and Ellen behind him. Another robber moved to where Billy had been standing and bent to pick up the sack. Katie saw his jacket sleeve rise up, revealing a distinctive birthmark. He pulled it down hastily, looking up to see if anyone had noticed. Katie cast her eyes to the ground, not wanting to meet his gaze. She continued to stare at the dusty ground until the robbers had mounted their horses and started to ride off. As soon as she heard the canter of the hooves, she ran toward the conductor.

He wasn't dead.

She pulled her jacket off and made it into a pillow for his head. She could see the blood spreading through his shirt.

"Thank ye kindly, Miss," the injured man whispered.

"Hush up, now. You need to preserve your strength." Katie watched as one of the male passengers checked the wound. He stood up, shaking his head. Her heart sank.

"Miss, could you do something for me?"

"Yes, of course."

"Please write my Annie and tell her I didn't suffer. She was all in a tither about me taking this trip. She thought I was too old. Happens she was right."

"I promise, but you can tell her yourself when you get better."

The old man smiled sadly before closing his eyes.

Katie sat there for a while, holding his hand, the tears streaming down her face. She could hear Ellen sobbing behind her. Why was the world so cruel?

CHAPTER 16

Daniel had never felt so helpless in his life. Without his gun, he couldn't do anything, but that didn't make standing there watching thieves shoot an innocent man any easier. He had felt the girl move and instinctively grabbed her arm. She wasn't from 'round here. She didn't know the types of men who held up trains.

Her outburst at the robber earned his admiration and annoyance in equal measure. How could she be so stupid and so brave? She, a mere girl of about twenty, had stood up to an armed raider. He shook his head. She probably had no idea how lucky she was the other robber had shouted at Billy. Train robbers were not known for treating womenfolk with respect.

As soon as the men had gone, he had moved to the

front of the train to see how fast they could get underway. The man who had been shot needed medical attention if he wasn't already dead. Daniel itched to get to Clover Springs. He intended to ride with the sheriff to track down these outlaws.

Thankfully, the robbers hadn't damaged the water tank too severely, so the train could limp to Clover Springs where it would have to be repaired. He helped some of the men move the rocks and timber blocking the tracks. Thank God the driver had seen the blockade in time to stop; otherwise, the train could have derailed, injuring more people.

Daniel walked to where a crowd of passengers had gathered. He saw the sisters at the center of the crowd, the older one holding the hand of the slain man. Tears ran down her cheeks, her lips moving in prayer. His fist clenched as he wished again he had kept his gun and could have put a bullet in Billy.

Gently, he tapped her on the shoulder.

"Please, Miss, stand up and take your sister back into the train car. There is nothing more you can do here."

She looked up at him, her violet eyes swimming with tears. "The poor man didn't have a chance, did he?"

Daniel shook his head before removing his jacket

and laying it over the conductor's face. They would need to move the body into the train, but he didn't want her to witness that. She had seen enough.

"Come on, Miss. The sooner you and the other passengers get into the cars, the quicker we will reach help."

He offered her his hand and helped her to her feet. She wobbled and instinctively he tightened his grip, pulling her slightly closer. She smelled faintly of roses. He quashed the urge to pull her tight against him. This was neither the time nor the place.

KATIE TRIED hard to get a grip on her emotions. The smell of gunshots and blood had taken her back to the day the soldiers came. Her body shook so badly as she relived the terror. She forced her eyes open. Breathe slowly. Ellen trembled beside her.

"Katie, that was horrible. I want to go back to Boston. I can't stay here. I am too…" Ellen stopped talking. She turned ghostly white before passing out.

"Ellen."

At Katie's cry of distress, Daniel whirled around, catching the younger girl before she fell. He carried her into the train car, laying her gently on one of the seats.

"Poor kid. She's terrified. I'll go get her a drink."

Katie rushed to Ellen's side. Gradually the young girl came round but lay crying quietly. Daniel returned, holding Katie's reticule and some water.

"Found it on the ground. I think they forgot to open it. Sorry but I couldn't find any brandy."

"Water's perfect. She's come around now but thank you, Mr…" Katie stammered realizing she didn't know his name.

"Daniel Sullivan." Daniel tipped his hat smiling but his eyes were troubled. Katie found herself rubbing his arm.

"She will be fine. Ellen's tougher than she looks. We both are. My name is Kathleen O'Callaghan but most call me Katie. Thank you, Mr. Sullivan, for protecting me earlier as well as looking after Ellen."

"Pleasure, Miss O'Callaghan, although remind me never to annoy you. That's some temper you have."

Katie opened her mouth to give him a smart reply but at his look, realized he was teasing her. She smiled despite wishing his name had been Mr. Cassidy.

Daniel's arm tingled from her touch. She was obviously as terrified as her younger sister but far too brave to admit it. He had an overwhelming urge to put his arms around her. He wanted to remove the terror from her eyes and kiss her senseless. The last few hours had shown how unpredictable life could be. It would be dangerous for them to continue their journey. Far safer to stay in the town where he could protect them both.

CHAPTER 17

When they finally reached Clover Springs, Daniel seemed reluctant to leave them alone, but she had assured him they would be fine. He had to go to the sheriff's office to volunteer for the posse who would ride out and try to catch the raiders.

"What will we do if the train can't be fixed?" Ellen asked.

Katie didn't answer. She needed to think. She wondered how much it would cost to send Mr. Cassidy a telegram.

"Mr. Sullivan is coming back," Ellen whispered.

Katie's stomach twisted at the sight of the man walking toward them. If only he was her intended. *Stop thinking like that. It won't help anyone.*

"Ladies, why are you still standing here? You should be resting," he asked.

Ellen shrugged her shoulders in a very unladylike fashion before announcing, "Katie isn't sure we have sufficient money to stay anywhere in town."

"Ellen," Katie hissed. She could strangle her sister sometimes. Their mother used to say Ellen only opened her mouth to change her feet. This was just typical. Katie saw Mr. Sullivan looking at her and she imagined his gaze was full of pity. She didn't need that from anyone, especially him.

"Please forgive my sister. We have sufficient funds, thanks to you returning my reticule."

Daniel nodded but stayed silent.

He is probably wondering why we're still standing there. Katie wasn't going to admit she had wanted to talk to him again.

"If the train has to be repaired, how long do you think it will be before we can continue our travels? We are supposed to get the stage from Whitewater to Clear Creek."

"I don't know, Miss O'Callaghan. A couple of days, I guess. Do you have family meeting you there?"

"Sort of. I am supposed to get married there on Friday."

. . .

DANIEL REACTED as if he had been stung. Married. Just his luck. To find a woman who made his senses beat faster than a rattlesnake bite, only for her to be promised to another.

"No chance of that happening today, Miss O'Callaghan." Surprise flared in her eyes at his gruff tone. He tried to temper it but the anger remained. "Just spoke to the train's fireman. The damage is worse than it seemed. It will take a couple of days at least. They also need to replace poor Mr. Smithson."

"Oh, I see. Yes, of course, that poor man. I must write the note to his wife like I promised."

She sounded panicky, but Daniel held back. She wasn't his problem. Not if she was going to married to someone else.

WHAT GOT INTO HIM? Why is he so angry? Katie bit her lip. *Maybe he feels responsible for us after what happened.* Well, she was a big girl and could take care of herself. But she was in a strange town. She risked a glance at him, hoping he would smile or say something, but he stayed silent. She hated to ask for more from him but she didn't have a choice. She took a deep breath and prayed her voice would be steady.

"Perhaps you could direct us to a boarding house where we may rest and change after the journey?"

"It would be my pleasure." Mr. Sullivan took his hat off and bowed. Katie bit back a retort. She supposed she deserved his rebuke for using a superior tone. Directness may be Ellen's failing, but being ornery was one Katie had in buckets.

"I do hope we are not putting you at an inconvenience, Mr. Sullivan."

"Not at all, Miss O'Callaghan. My mother will be delighted to meet you."

"Your mother? Perhaps you misunderstood. We didn't invite ourselves to your home. Despite what my sister said earlier, we do have funds. We are looking for a house open to paying guests."

Mr. Sullivan laughed but it wasn't a happy sound. Irritated beyond belief, she was tempted to tell him to take a hike. But she couldn't. She had to think of Ellen.

"My mother runs a boarding house. She opened it after my father died. She didn't fancy staying on the ranch outside of town, so she gave that to my older brother. She guessed the railroad would bring travelers needing suitable accommodation. I assure you it is respectable and somewhere your mother, if she were traveling with you, would feel comfortable staying.

"Our mother is —" Ellen snapped her mouth shut in response to Katie's pinch. She rubbed her arm, glaring at her older sister.

"Thank you very much, Mr. Sullivan. We are much obliged. Come on, Ellen." Katie took Ellen's arm, forcibly dragging her down the street. She didn't want to spend any more time with Mr. Sullivan than absolutely necessary. Mr. Sullivan picked up their bags with ease and walked down the steps of the station onto the street.

Katie looked around at the town Mr. Smithson had spoken so highly of. Thankfully, it was a dry day so the street was only dusty. *It must get real muddy when it's raining,* Katie thought as she picked up her skirt to avoid walking into fresh horse dung.

She hoped the boarding house would have a bath. She was desperate to be clean again after the long journey. Mr. Sullivan pointed out a couple of buildings to them. They passed a large mercantile, the goods on display in the window causing Ellen to stop and stare. A restaurant and small hotel was situated on the corner. She thought it might be the boarding house, but Mr. Sullivan kept walking. He didn't make conversation. Katie was glad, as it gave her time to get her thoughts in order. Would Mr. Cassidy be concerned when they didn't arrive on schedule? Would he think to check for a telegram? Maybe the stage driver would have heard about the train robbery and tell him? Or would that be old news around here in a few days? Nellie's voice popped into her head, saying it depends on how many murders they have this far west.

As they walked further away from the station, they passed a saloon, thankfully on the other side of the street. Some cowboys exiting the doors stopped and stared at them. A couple of the men made a few undesirable comments, causing the rest to laugh coarsely. Katie stiffened and walked straighter, taking Ellen's hand in the process. "Look straight in front of you. Pretend they aren't there," she hissed to her sister. Mr. Sullivan stopped, letting them walk slightly ahead of him. Katie saw him give the saloon guests a look, which thankfully silenced them. She was sure the men would have approached them had they been unaccompanied. "Thank you, Mr. Sullivan."

"You are very welcome, Ma'am," he replied, continuing to walk.

Ma'am! Just how old does he think I am? Katie glanced in a window as she passed. Sure, she was dirty from the trip, but the experience hadn't aged her that much, had it?

CHAPTER 18

They kept walking down what she assumed, was the main street. A small distance away stood a white church and near it was what she presumed was the schoolhouse, as it wasn't yet completed. Just past it, she saw a pretty white clapboard building with flowers on either side of the door. The windows sparkled in the sunshine. There was a small sign saying Sullivan's boarding house. It looked so pretty and inviting, Katie couldn't help smiling.

Mr. Sullivan stopped, putting their bags on the porch. He opened the door, calling for his mother.

"Daniel. You're back. Let me look at you."

A middle-aged woman with dark hair streaked with gray hugged the young man. Only then did she see Ellen and Katie standing there.

"Please excuse my mother. It's been at least a week since she last saw me."

Mrs. Sullivan blushed before swatting her son out of her way.

"These ladies have traveled a long way and need somewhere to stay, so I brought them here."

"Where else would you bring them?" Mrs. Sullivan laughed. "I am so sorry, girls. Daniel's right. He was only away for a week this time, but before that he was away for years and I am just making up for all the lost hugs." Mrs. Sullivan came toward them with her arms open. Katie thought she was going to hug them, too, but she didn't. She shook their hands as Katie introduced herself first and then Ellen. "Please come in. Welcome to our little town. You must be exhausted."

Mrs. Sullivan and her boarding house were just as nice as Daniel had said. She showed both of them up to a large room overlooking the rear of the property.

"I think you will find it quieter. The rooms at the front of the house overlook the street. It can get a little rowdy, especially if the men venture down this direction after the saloon has closed." Mrs. Sullivan's disapproval of this behavior was evident from her facial expression.

"It is lovely, thank you," Katie said happily, glancing around the room. Although sparsely furnished, the linen on the large bed was crisp and white.

"I guess you girls will want to wash up for supper. I will send Daniel up with the bath. I put water on to boil earlier for some sheets, but you look like you would benefit from it more. Supper won't be on the table until six, so you have time for a nap should you wish to rest."

"That would be lovely. Thank you, Mrs. Sullivan."

"She's very nice, isn't she, Katie? I hope your new home is as nice as this," said Ellen after Mrs. Sullivan closed the door.

They shared the bathwater but didn't linger, as the longing for a real bed overcame them.

HAVING RESTED FOR A WHILE, they both felt better and soon hunger drove them downstairs. The lovely smells coming from what they presumed was the kitchen made their mouths water. Mrs. Sullivan seated them in the dining room. There weren't any other guests around. Looking at the clock, Katie realized they must have slept longer than she had thought.

"I'm sorry, Mrs. Sullivan. You should have called us when you served the other guests."

"Don't you worry about that. You and your sister needed a rest after everything you had been through today. Daniel told me what happened before he rode out with the sheriff. I hope they catch those varmints."

She served them each a roast dinner, the plate piled high with meat, vegetables, potatoes and gravy.

"I am just going to finish tidying up in the kitchen. Elizabeth usually helps when a train comes in, but her young'un is feeling poorly. I will be right back to see if you want anything else."

"Thank you, Mrs. Sullivan," the girls chorused before starting to eat.

They had just finished when Mrs. Sullivan came back, cleared their dinner dishes, and set two plates of apple pie and cream on the table. She poured three cups of coffee.

"Do you mind if I join you? I am parched, but I hate drinking coffee on my own."

"Of course, please sit. Thank you for the lovely food. We haven't eaten so well in a long time," Katie said while Ellen nodded, her mouth too full of pie to speak.

The girls ate as Mrs. Sullivan told them a little about Clover Springs. "I am so glad you met Daniel on the train. He is my middle son. His older brother David, or Davy as we call him, lives out on the ranch, and my youngest, Brian, is away at school. He's set on becoming a lawyer. Daniel will take over the mercantile when Mr. Brook goes back East to his daughter."

Katie tried to imagine Daniel working in a store. He didn't seem the type. Instead, she could see him working with horses. His body was so trim yet muscular. Her cheeks heated as she thought of the way her body had tingled when he had taken her elbow. She wondered how it would feel to kiss him. She took a deep breath as Ellen's chatter pierced her thoughts.

"Katie has come to be a mail order bride," Ellen volunteered, looking at her plate as if she wanted to pick it up and lick up the crumbs.

Katie kicked her sister under the table. When was she going to learn to be discreet?

"A mail order bride in Clover Springs? Do I know the lucky man?"

"My groom to be is a man called Mr. Montis Cassidy, but he isn't from here. He lives on a ranch near Clear Creek. We were supposed to take the train to the next station and from there take a stage to Clear Creek. But after today..." Katie couldn't continue. Her eyes filled up with tears, and Mrs. Sullivan took her hand to give it a little squeeze.

"You must have been so frightened. Those men are savages, gunning down an innocent man like that. Mr. Smithson was a lovely man. He used to call in here for his dinner occasionally."

"I was terrified, but our Katie was brave as usual. She wanted to go help the conductor, but your son stopped her. I am so glad he did, as I didn't like those men. They looked at us as if they wanted to eat us."

Katie met Mrs. Sullivan's eyes above Ellen's head. Her sister didn't really understand what could have happened, but she was astute enough to realize it wouldn't have been pleasant. Katie pushed her chair back from the table and went to her sister, wrapping her arm around Ellen's shoulders, holding her as she cried.

"Come on, darling girl. Let's get to bed. It's been a long day. Thank you very much for a lovely meal, Mrs. Sullivan."

"It was my pleasure, girls. I trust you will sleep well."

Ellen cried herself to sleep, leaving Katie awake through the early hours of the night. She sat by the window, looking up at the clear night sky. It reminded her of home.

She didn't want to think about home. Her thoughts strayed once more to Daniel Sullivan, but she didn't think that was proper. She forced herself to think positively about her reason for making this trip. On Friday, she was supposed to wed Montis Cassidy and start a new life with her husband and sister. But how would she get to Clear Creek?

She wondered where his ranch was in relation to Clover Springs. He hadn't mentioned the exact location, only that it was a decent size and he was hoping to expand. She had written of her experience on the farm in Galway. The farm back home bore little resemblance to any land holding she had encountered on their trip west.

Her thoughts flicked back to Daniel Sullivan. He wouldn't be a ranch owner but a trader. In town. She wanted to live on a farm. Wasn't that what she had told Mrs. Gantley? What did it matter where Daniel Sullivan was employed? Annoyed, she gave herself a mental shake. All this excitement about robbers and Daniel Sullivan would soon be ancient history. Wouldn't it?

The next morning, Katie left Ellen chatting to Mrs. Sullivan, who had agreed to look after the younger girl, giving Katie a chance to send her telegram to the office in Clear Creek.

I hope he thinks to go check the post. She explained in as few words as possible that they were stuck in Clover Springs. She asked Mr. Cassidy what she should do next. She didn't know if she could catch a stage from Clover Springs to him or if he would ride over to her. She hoped he would reply quickly. She didn't know how much the boarding house would cost. Would she have enough money to last until Mr. Cassidy answered?

CHAPTER 19

CLEAR CREEK

Montis kicked the dirt. The stage was late. He had better things to be doing than waiting around the town. He looked over at the saloon. Did he have time to go get a drink? Maybe that wasn't the best idea. No decent girl would want to meet her husband-to-be for the first time and have him stinking of whiskey. Lord. She hadn't even arrived yet and already he was changing his ways to please her. Darn it anyway.

He stomped over to the saloon and ordered a whiskey. "What you doing all dressed up, Montis?" The barkeep stopped teasing at the look he received and silently filled up the empty glass. Then another. Still no sign of the stage. Eventually, about an hour or so had gone by before Montis heard the distinctive shouts of Fred, the stage driver. He downed his last drink and headed outside.

"You're late."

"You work that out all by yourself, Montis?" Fred said sarcastically.

"No need to get uppity. I've been waiting and there are chores to be done at home. Nobody else going to see to them. What kept ya?"

"The axle broke. We had to change a wheel. You think you had problems. At least you got to have a drink. My throat thinks the well has gone dry."

Montis was only half listening to Fred moaning. His attention was fixed on the occupants of the stage. The only woman passenger looked to be about thirty and a proper school marm at that. Had the girl lied in her letter? She said she was young.

Virgil, I am going to kill you for this. Montis swallowed hard before stepping forward, only to be nearly knocked over by another man who reached the lady first.

"Mildred, at last you arrived. I thought you would never come."

"I'd have come a lot sooner if you had sent me the proper fare, but I can just guess where you have been spending your dollars. I see you been in the saloon again. What's her name this time?"

"Now, Mildred, don't be harsh. I've missed you

something fierce. Come along now and see the little house I got for you."

"Little!" The woman's screech caused all the men to stare at her. Her husband blushed. Montis stepped back. She sounded just like his ma. With relief, he watched the man take the woman's arm and walk her purposefully away from the direction of the saloon.

Montis stood for a few minutes before turning his attention back to the stage. He even looked inside to confirm there was nobody hiding in it.

"What you done with my bride?" he said to Fred.

"Your what?" Fred's eyes nearly burst out of his face.

"You heard. I had a bride coming all the way from Boston, only she's not here. Did you lose her?" Montis glared at Fred, not liking the way he was laughing at him.

"How much whiskey have you had? Lose a passenger? In all my years of driving the stage, when have I ever lost anything? Maybe she decided not to come. Got sense like."

Montis bristled, his fists clenching. No man would ever dare to speak to him like that. *When Virgil was around*. He rounded on Fred, but the stagecoach driver stood his ground.

"When's the next stage due?"

"Won't be here till a week on Friday. Are you sure

you got your dates right?" At the look from Montis, Fred tried again. "You checked the telegraph office? Maybe your lady friend done sent you a note."

Montis cursed. Why hadn't he thought of that? *Because you're not Virgil. You're the dumb one.* He turned and marched off down the street, the sound of Fred's laughter ringing in his ears. That's all he needed. Not only would the whole of Clear Creek know he'd been waiting on a woman, but they would know he'd ordered a bride like you would a parcel in the post. Why couldn't life ever be plain sailing? He thought all he had to do was meet her off the stage, take her over to the preacher and then take her back to the ranch tonight. He knew getting married was a stupid idea. A real dumb thing to do.

CHAPTER 20

Katie got out of bed carefully, not wanting to disturb Ellen. Dressing quickly, she went downstairs to ask Mrs. Sullivan what time the telegraph office would open. It had been three days, surely long enough to get a reply from Mr. Cassidy. She found her sitting at the kitchen table, her head in her hands.

"Are you all right, Mrs. Sullivan?" Katie asked, although the answer was obvious. Her host's face was unnaturally rosy.

"Oh, good morning, Katie. I'm sorry. I should be fixing breakfast, but my legs don't seem to want to work this morning." As if to prove her point, she rose but seemed to fall forward. Katie grabbed her in time, putting her arm around her waist to help support her back toward the chair.

"You sit here. I will go get help. I won't be a minute." Katie tried to smile reassuringly, but she couldn't keep the worry from her tone. She ran upstairs to wake Ellen. It didn't take her sister long to dress and between them they escorted Mrs. Sullivan back to her room.

"Lie down and rest. You will soon feel much better." Katie set a glass of cool water beside the bed. "Ellen, sponge her head every few minutes. I am going to cook breakfast for the guests. I will be back as soon as I can."

Ellen nodded. With a house full of brothers and sisters, they were both well versed in dealing with fevers and other ailments. Katie raced back downstairs. She wasn't sure how many guests were booked and expecting breakfast. There was no time to waste.

Mrs. Sullivan had already put biscuits in the oven and they were just browning nicely. Katie cooked some bacon and scrambled eggs. All she needed now was some butter and molasses.

"Ma, I sure missed your cooking. Something smells mighty good."

Katie's heart soared at the sound of his voice. *He was back.* She pushed her hair back from her face, hoping it wasn't covered in flour.

"You're not Ma."

Katie laughed at the obvious statement before

saying quickly, "Mrs. Sullivan wasn't feeling well so I sent her back to bed. She was worried about breakfast, so I—"

"You did all this? But you are a guest."

"There was nobody else to do it, and I guessed you didn't want a house full of hungry guests. It was no different to the cooking I did in Boston." Only there, she had a pump in the kitchen and a better stove, but she didn't think it would help to point out the deficiencies in the kitchen.

"It was very kind of you, Miss O'Callaghan, but you are a paying guest. I will take over now."

"You?" Katie couldn't keep the surprise from her voice.

"Why not? I've helped Ma once or twice before."

Katie stared pointedly at his whiskers before moving down to his hands.

"Your mother has a reputation to uphold. I don't think the female guests would appreciate a cowboy serving breakfast." *Not even one as gorgeous as you.*

The look he gave her made her think she had spoken her thoughts out loud. She swallowed hard and looked at the floor, hoping he would attribute her rosy cheeks to the heat of the kitchen.

He laughed and her stomach somersaulted once more.

"Okay, you win, Miss O'Callaghan, but do you

think the ladies may object to me eating some of that fine breakfast?"

"To be sure they won't."

As he turned toward the door to the dining room, she added, "Not so long as you wash up first."

She giggled at the look he sent her before the slight smell of burning had her racing to the oven to rescue the biscuits.

* * *

"Wash up indeed," Daniel huffed. He had a bath last night when the posse got back to town. They should have still been chasing the raiders, but one of the men took sick and then his horse lost a shoe. It looked like the gang had taken to the mountains. Sheriff Matthews had ordered them all back to town to gather proper provisions, warmer clothes and also to round up more men. They would head out again in a few days when extra men had been drafted from some of the neighboring towns. The railroad had offered a large reward to be shared amongst the volunteers riding with the sheriff. *Won't need the bank loan if we capture those varmints.* But it wasn't just the lure of the money. Daniel liked Clover Springs and didn't want the type of trouble those men would bring to this town.

He looked down at his hands. They looked clean enough to him. *Maybe I've been on the trail too long.*

It would certainly explain his urge to touch Miss O'Callaghan every time he saw her. He had to count to ten to stop himself from reaching out to wipe a flour trail from her cheek. She looked so pretty standing at Ma's cooker.

Ma? He had been so caught up with thoughts of Katie he hadn't thought about what was wrong with his mother. Cursing under his breath, he ran back into the house, taking the stairs two steps at a time.

After seeing how poorly she was, Daniel sent for the doctor, who insisted Mrs. Sullivan stay in bed.

"I can't stay in bed. Elizabeth is looking after her young'un. There is nobody to look after my guests."

"Seems to me that the young Irish girls are managing quite nicely. There was such a divine smell downstairs, I am going to ask you to invite me to stay for breakfast," the doctor said.

"The Irish girls? But they are supposed to be guests. I have to get up." Mrs. Sullivan went to sit up but swayed and fell back onto the pillow.

"Ma, stop being a stubborn old woman and listen to the doc. He knows best." Daniel looked at the doctor, who nodded. His mother didn't look too convinced. He had to find a different way to persuade her.

"You'd be doing those girls a favor. They weren't expecting to stay in a boarding house. Maybe they would be happy to look after the place in exchange for food and lodgings for a few days. Just until you get back on your feet."

"Wouldn't be Christian not to help those young girls. They don't look old enough to be traveling across the country by themselves," the doctor added, winking at Daniel.

"Well, I guess you are right. Please ask them, but mind your manners, son. These are nice girls and you've been on the trail a long time."

"Yes, Ma," Daniel said grumpily. *What do you think I am going to do, kiss her senseless?* Daniel grinned despite himself. Maybe Ma knew him well after all.

He pulled the colorful quilt covers up over his mother and surprised both of them by giving her a gentle kiss on the forehead.

CHAPTER 21

Katie spent the day getting used to the routine at the boarding house. Mrs. Sullivan had a number of guests who were stuck waiting for the trains to get back to normal. Ellen had helped her to bake bread, pies and biscuits. Katie saw to the meals. Mrs. Sullivan kept the larder well stocked. Daniel had gone to the store and brought back some additional foodstuffs. In addition to cooking, they also had to strip the bedrooms some guests had vacated and prepare them for the next visitors.

Katie was wondering how to get the laundry done when Daniel came into the kitchen.

"Any coffee going for a tired working man?"

Katie looked around her. "Where is he?"

"Who?"

"The working man?" Katie giggled at the look on Daniel's face as he realized she was teasing.

"Careful, Miss O'Callaghan, or you just may end up biting off more than you can chew."

She watched as he picked up a freshly baked cookie. "These sure smell tasty." As if in agreement, his stomach rumbled loudly, causing both of them to burst out laughing. "My apologies, Miss. Good thing Ma is in bed or she would be taking the switch to me."

Katie smiled, but the mention of Mrs. Sullivan reminded her of the need for laundry. "Mr. Sullivan, would you mind showing me where your mother keeps her laundry supplies? There is some washing to be done."

"Ma sends that out to a local woman. Says her back can't take the scrubbing. I can show you where she's at if you like. I have to go see the sheriff anyway."

"Thank you kindly. Please give me a few minutes."

Daniel nodded, sitting down with the plate of cookies and pouring himself another coffee.

Katie gathered the dirty linen into a bundle. She wasn't sure how she was going to carry the load down the street. Maybe Mrs. Sullivan had a basket. Daniel would know.

She threw a quick glance in the mirror. Her hair was escaping from the bun she had fashioned that morning. She pushed it back, wishing she had time to go to her room and start over, but she didn't want to keep him waiting. Was it proper for the two of them to go walking? She was betrothed to another. Maybe she should ask Ellen to come with them. *We are walking through a town. It's not as if we are going to be alone. He is just showing me the way to the laundry woman.*

Katie shook her head. Maybe the sun was getting to her and addling her brain. She picked up her bonnet and ran back downstairs toward the kitchen. Daniel had the basket waiting and once filled, he picked it up as if it were weightless. *He has nice shoulders.* Flustered, Katie dropped her reticule. He pushed the door open and waited until she was outside before following.

They walked back toward the main street of town with Daniel pointing out places of interest.

"Why did you decide to move out West?"

Katie paused. What should she say? She didn't really want to admit to being a mail order bride. Why not? There was no shame in it, was there? *But what if he thinks I am desperate? He'd be right.*

"I answered an ad in the paper. We were staying with relatives and it wasn't working out too well. I don't like living in big cities. I want to live in the open where I can breathe."

"Well, you certainly came to the right place. If it's one thing Colorado Territory has, it's lots of space. People think it's just mountains, but we have big wide-open prairies too. You would have seen that from the train."

"Yes, at times you didn't see anything else, just acres and acres of grass. You said your brother lives on a ranch."

"He sure does. Pa grew up here. His father was one of the first settlers. He started Clover Springs with a few others. Mr. Brook, the old man who owns the mercantile, can tell you stories about my grandpa. I never met him. Pa died a couple of years back, and Davy, my older brother, took over the running of the ranch. Ma says it was too much hard work at her age, but I think she was lonesome. Anyway, she wanted to be nearer Elizabeth. She's my sister. She reminds me a little of you."

Katie smiled. She liked the sound of his voice and the way he talked, as if they had known each other forever and not for a few days.

"Yeah, she has a temper just like yours. You don't get on her wrong side. She stirs up crazier than a bee's nest."

Katie stopped walking and stood with her hands on her hips. "I, sir, do not have a temper."

Daniel didn't take offense. He laughed, and when she threw him a dirty look, he just got worse. "See, you do. There you go. You should have bright red hair, not hair the color of midnight."

He had stopped laughing and was staring down at her. Being tall for a girl, looking up into a man's face was an unusual experience. *Looking at one laughing at me is, too.*

SHE WANTED TO BE CROSS, but something in his eyes made her feel different. She felt the heat in his stare, her skin tingling as his eyes bored into hers. She fought an urge to move closer to him. She tore her eyes away and started walking. She had to say something to distract herself. "Where does this lady live? Are we nearly there?"

"Mrs. Kauffman lives on the next street. Don't be surprised if she invites you in for coffee. She loves to meet all the new people who arrive in town. She is a nice lady and is doing her best to get by. Her husband was killed in the mine a few years ago. Ma and a few of the other townsfolk make sure to give her enough work to keep food on the table for her and the young'uns."

Wonder if he is sweet on her? Why would you care, Katie O'Callaghan?

"It was like that back in Galway. If anyone needed help, the other women looked out for one another. Best they could, anyway."

"Makes sense. If we share what we got, we all

prosper that bit more. Here we are. I will leave the basket with you. Are you okay with finding your way back to Ma's?"

Katie nodded. She seemed to have lost the ability to speak and think at the same time.

"I got to find out when the sheriff wants to go looking for those raiders. Then I need to go out to see Davy. I might stay the night, so please tell Ma not to worry if she doesn't see me before breakfast." Katie nodded, not wanting to acknowledge the disappointment his words caused. He wouldn't be there for dinner.

Daniel deposited the basket at the door, and with a laugh and a bow, he strode off down the street. Katie stared after him. She had never met anyone who had the same effect on her as he did. She wanted to spend all day looking at him, listening to him speak and laugh. *I hope Mr. Cassidy makes me laugh like Daniel does.* The door of the house opened and a young hassled-looking woman came out holding a blonde toddler on her hip. "Sorry to keep you waiting. The young'un won't settle for me."

"She is very pretty." Katie smiled at the little one, who hid her face in her ma's shoulder. "Mrs. Sullivan isn't feeling too well today. She asked me to bring you the linen."

"Oh, poor lady. I hope she be better soon. Tell her

they will be ready tomorrow evening, if that isn't too late."

Katie had forgotten to check when Mrs. Sullivan expected the linen, but she found herself nodding. "Will I call back for it tomorrow?"

"That would be fine. Perhaps you could stop and have coffee? I would ask you in today, but I am worried the little one might be poorly. I don't want you catching anything."

"Thank you kindly, but I have other chores to finish. I will see you tomorrow. Goodbye, little one. I hope you feel better soon."

The toddler gave Katie a quick smile before hiding her face in her mother's shoulder once more.

CHAPTER 22

He hadn't spent long with the sheriff so he had made it out to Davy's in time for dinner. Mrs. Higgins had outdone herself again but Daniel was too wound up to eat.

"What's got into you? Not usual for you to turn down a meal."

"Sorry, Davy, but I got a lot on my mind. Ma is sick and I didn't want to worry her. I didn't tell her the full story about the visit with the bank."

Davy sat straighter in his chair.

"Did they turn you down?"

"Not exactly, Davy. They said yes."

"What's got you looking like you got a bellyache?"

"It's a condition of the loan that I get married. The banker seems to think I ride on my brains. He said it's just a matter of time before I head off into the mountains looking for gold."

Davy spat out his coffee as he burst out laughing. He swallowed quickly at the look his brother gave him.

"The banker doesn't know you, Daniel. We both know how often strangers come to town claiming to have discovered the next big strike. They hand out small gold nuggets or silver pieces in the saloon tempting those who should know better. If you were to listen to some, the rivers on the mountain are golden or silver-colored, not made of plain old water. Every dreamer from here to Denver believes he will be the next one to make it rich.

"I have no interest in mining for gold. I have had enough of the harsh reality of sleeping out under the stars."

"I know that but the banker doesn't. He thinks like most big city folk. You just need to prove him wrong."

"That's easier said than done."

"I didn't figure you for a quitter, Daniel."

"Well, unless you been hiding someone, I don't see any young single females around Clover Springs, do you? There isn't a suitable single female between here and Clear Creek." Daniel shook his head as his thoughts shifted to Katie. She was infinitely marriageable. *She is also engaged, you oaf.*

"You still want the store, don't you?" At Daniel's nod, Davy continued. "I wish I had the money to give you but everything is tied up in the ranch. You will just have to find a wife."

"So how do you suggest I do that, dear brother?"

"Don't you listen to the preacher every Sunday? The Good Lord will provide."

Daniel looked at Davy. He couldn't work out if his brother was joshing with him or was serious. He didn't really believe praying for a wife would work but it couldn't do any harm? Maybe he should put an ad in one of those matrimonial guides anyway. It wouldn't hurt to give the Lord a helping hand.

* * *

ONCE BACK AT the boarding house, Katie was relieved to find Mrs. Sullivan sleeping more peacefully. Her fever seemed to be lower than before. Whatever ailed her wasn't serious. She would make a full recovery.

Dinner went well. She and Ellen worked as a team – all those months entertaining Uncle Joseph's guests had a purpose after all. God did work in mysterious ways.

When they had cleaned up after dinner, the dishes done and put away and the stove banked up for the night, they crept up to bed and fell asleep almost as soon as their heads hit the pillow. For the first time in a long time, Katie slept through until morning.

Breakfast went as well as dinner with a number of the guests complimenting the sisters on the food and comfortable accommodation. Katie heard Ellen tell some of the guests who were leaving to tell their friends about Clover Springs' finest boarding house. She smiled. It was about time Ellen came out of her shell and returned to the girl she had been in Ireland. *Mam would be proud of her.* Katie took a tray up to Mrs. Sullivan. She was awake and sitting up as Katie pushed the door open and entered the bedroom.

"Katie—I hope you don't mind me calling you that —thank you so much for everything. I don't know what I would have done if you and Ellen hadn't been here."

"We're glad to help. How are you feeling?"

"Much better. Thank you, dear. I hope to be up later today." At a look from Katie, Mrs. Sullivan said, "Maybe tomorrow would be better."

Katie nodded her head in agreement. They spent a couple of minutes talking about lunch. Katie told Mrs. Sullivan of her visit to Mrs. Kaufmann.

"That poor woman. All alone with two young'uns at her age. She is barely twenty."

"She is very pretty. Maybe she will find a new

husband?" Katie said, wondering if Mrs. Sullivan had thought about finding a wife for Daniel.

"She certainly is. I don't know why she hasn't married again. If it's one thing we are not short of here in Clover Springs, it's single men. Speaking of which, do you know if Daniel is back yet?"

Katie shook her head before excusing herself. She didn't want to talk about Daniel. Mrs. Sullivan may be feeling poorly, but she didn't trust herself not to give her feelings away. She liked Daniel more than she had a right to, given her promise to another man.

CHAPTER 23

"What are you staring at?

"You missed a bit. That plate still has gravy on it." Daniel smirked. "As you said often enough, Ma has standards."

Katie's face flushed. She couldn't believe he had caught her being less than completely thorough. Imagine what a guest would think if they were served a dirty plate. She took up the gleaming plate; there wasn't a spot on it. She looked up in time to catch his teasing glance.

"Why, you … you …"

"Cat got your tongue, Miss O'Callaghan?"

Irritated beyond belief, Katie flicked some dirty dishwater at him. *Oh, I shouldn't have done that.* His eyes widened. She took a step back as he made a grab for the dishcloth she now held behind her back.

Eyes gleaming, he reached around her waist for the cloth.

Her body stilled. She was barely able to breathe as she became aware of his nearness. It wasn't just his muscular body, but his scent enveloped her. Her mouth dried as she tried to ignore the sensations his nearness was causing. She licked her lips, trying to find her voice to tell him to let her go, but she couldn't get the words out. She risked a glance at him to see if he felt something, too. His eyes were glazed, bluer than usual as he looked down at her. Rather than release her, he pulled her closer. His lips came nearer to hers as she closed her eyes. Any second now, she would taste him.

Mr. Cassidy. Flushing even more, she pushed against Daniel's body. She couldn't let him kiss her, much as she wanted it to happen. She couldn't risk him knowing how she felt. That was her secret. She threw the cloth in the direction of the sink and ran for safety.

DANIEL STOOD at the sink staring after her. He could still feel the press of her body against his, her chest rising and falling rapidly as she struggled to breathe. The heat between them threatened to devour him. She had felt it, too. That's why she had run off. The last thing he wanted was for her to be afraid. He needed to go after her to apologize, but first he needed to cool off. A dip in the creek should do it.

* * *

Katie was skittish all day. A couple of times she had snapped at Ellen, leaving her sister as nervous as she was. Every time the door banged, she stilled, waiting to hear his voice. When it wasn't him, she was disappointed, although she knew she should also be relieved. He hadn't returned by the time she escorted Ellen up the stairs to their bedroom.

"I'm sorry Ellen, my darling girl, for being so argumentative today. I guess I am nervous."

"About the wedding. That's understandable. I saw Daniel earlier. He looked cross, too. I wonder what he's worried about?"

Katie didn't want to discuss Daniel. Not now and especially not with Ellen. She leaned over and gave her sister a kiss on the forehead. "Sweet dreams, Ellen."

She headed back down the stairs, intent on finishing up the chores in the kitchen. The fire had been banked and the last of the dishes put away. She was just about to head to bed when the door opened and closed gently. Without looking up, she knew he was back. Frantically, she looked for an escape route, but he stood between her and the door.

"Miss O'Callaghan, I apologize."

"There's no need. Goodnight, Mr. Sullivan." Katie looked pointedly over his shoulder at the door.

"I'm hungry. Sit with me while I eat?"

"There is food on the stove. It should be warm enough. Now if you will excuse me, I'm tired."

"Goodnight, Miss O'Callaghan."

Disconcerted by the fact he still hadn't moved out of the way, Katie looked up. He had an awkward smile on his face. She raised an eyebrow questioningly.

"Please, Katie, hear me out. I'm sorry I manhandled you earlier. It wasn't my intention to frighten you. I was only playing with you."

"Playing? With what? My feelings? Let me tell you this, Mr. Sullivan, I am not interested in you. I am getting married. To a decent, God fearing man who I would hope wouldn't be kissing another man's fiancé."

"Kissing? We didn't get to that part." Daniel smirked.

Mortified, Katie bolted for the door. She couldn't believe she had effectively told him she thought about kissing him. Oh, Lord, what must he think of me?

"Miss O'Callaghan, do you accept my apology?"

Katie stopped. Without turning, she said coldly "I

accept your apology, Mr. Sullivan, now please, excuse me. It's late and I have a wedding to prepare for. "

As she closed the door, she could have sworn he said, "Of course, how could we forget?" What did he mean by that?

CHAPTER 24

Katie looked around the small dining room.

The table was set for lunch. She had washed and dried the breakfast dishes and put rabbit stew on a low heat to serve later. There was nothing left to do but go to the telegraph office and see if the reply was there. Sighing, she put on her coat just as Ellen came down the stairs.

"How is Mrs. Sullivan?" asked Katie.

"She's sleeping. Daniel is sitting with her. Where are you going, Katie?"

Daniel. She hadn't seen him since their encounter last night. She wondered if he was hungry. *It's his house. He knows where the food is kept.* She realized Ellen was looking at her curiously, waiting for an answer.

"Just down to the mercantile. I will be back shortly."

"I'll come with you."

"No, me darling girl, wait here. Just in case a guest comes in and needs something. I won't be long."

Katie steeled herself against the disappointment on the younger girl's face. She wanted space to read the telegram herself.

It was a beautiful day, the sky a clear blue with no sign of clouds. Although early, the sun was shining brightly as Katie adjusted her bonnet. She walked slowly down the main street, thinking again how pretty the little town was. She kept away from the saloon, but there wasn't anyone around. It was a bit early. She met a couple of people on the street who nodded and said hello.

On impulse, she decided to go into the mercantile and buy her sister some candy. She walked up the steps, stamping her feet a little to kick off the dust of the street. As she pushed the door, a little bell tinkled.

"I will be right with you," a man's voice called from the back of the store. She waited, looking around the shelves in wonder. It was like an Aladdin's cave full of treasure. She went over to the cloth, her fingers itching to feel the beautiful fabrics on display.

The bell tinkled again as an older woman strode into the store. She looked around, her gaze sweeping

Katie from top to bottom. Katie shivered in spite of herself. She wished she had changed before leaving the house, although her other dress wasn't much better than the one she stood in. She didn't imagine it would gain the other woman's approval either.

"Good morning, Mrs. Grey, and how are you this fine day?"

"I would be better if I was not kept waiting, Mr. Brook."

Katie gasped. The lady was so rude. She looked at the storekeeper, wondering what his response would be.

"I am so sorry to keep you from your busy day, Mrs. Grey, but I am afraid I will have to ask you to wait a little longer. This young lady came in first."

Katie stifled a laugh at the look of disbelief on Mrs. Grey's face. When Mr. Brook turned and winked at her, she couldn't help but laugh, turning it into a cough as Mrs. Grey focused her glare.

"Could I please have two peppermint sticks?"

"Of course you can, young lady. How do you like our little town?"

"It's lovely. Real pretty."

At the humph sounds behind her, Katie tried to speed up but only succeeded in letting the pennies in her hand fall to the floor. "Oh, I am so sorry. I am not usually so clumsy."

"I doubt that. Your kind can't help being stupid."

Katie couldn't help but stare at Mrs. Grey, who rather than apologize for her remark, simply stared back. Completely flustered, Katie wished she could reply, but Mam had always told them to respect their elders. She couldn't walk out either, as she didn't want to be rude to the storekeeper. She glanced at him again to apologize. He handed her a little bag. "Please take this as a welcome gift to our town. I will find your coins when I sweep up. Call back in later and I will return them to you."

"Thank you very much, sir."

"No need for thanks. A smile like yours is enough to brighten any man's day. Make sure to call back later. Now, Mrs. Grey, what can I do for you?"

Katie risked a look at the other woman. Mrs. Grey's face had turned red. She looked as if she was about to burst at the seams.

"After all the business I have given to you, Mr. Brook, over the years and you see fit to serve that... that..."

"Now, Mrs. Grey, don't upset yourself. You know what your heart is like. Do you have a list of what you need?"

Katie smiled widely as she left the store, listening to Mr. Brook smooth out Mrs. Grey's ruffles. She had no idea what she had done to upset the other woman, having only met her, but she knew one thing, Mrs. Grey's heart wasn't in danger. A stone couldn't break, now could it? *Katie O'Callaghan, think Christian thoughts.*

SHE MET a couple of other women as she walked down the street. They all seemed friendly. Thank goodness for that. Mrs. Grey wasn't a true reflection of the people of the town. She smiled at the man in the telegraph office, but her face fell when he handed her the piece of paper.

WILL ARRIVE AT CLOVER SPRINGS FRIDAY AT NOON. GET PREACHER. MONTIS.

Friday? How were they supposed to manage until then? She had some money, but staying in the boarding house for the next five days would eat into her savings very quickly.

CHAPTER 25

Katie frowned. Her fiancé didn't seem too bothered about how she would manage. All he could do was order her around. Find a preacher indeed. What about how are you doing for money or where are you staying? Men! She wasn't expecting declarations of love. It wasn't that type of marriage, but surely some consideration for their comfort was to be expected. She glanced at the telegram again, her sense of unease making her uncomfortable. Well, there was nothing she could do about it now. He was coming to get married and she best go book the preacher.

She had spotted the white church the first day when Daniel had shown them around the town. Daniel. She couldn't think of him now. She walked purposefully up to the church, climbed three steps and walked in. It wasn't a bit like the Catholic churches she was used to. There was no holy water for her to dip her finger in, but she still crossed herself. She walked in slowly, taking note of the absence of pictures of Our Lady and crucifixes. In their place were a couple of plain crosses and the heavenly smell of wild flowers. Contrary to what her uncle had said, her heels didn't catch fire as she walked further into the building. She didn't spot the preacher at first. He was kneeling on the floor.

"Excuse me, sir?" *What did you call a preacher?*

To her dismay, he bumped his head as he scrambled off the floor.

"Oh, I am so sorry. Are you hurt?" She rushed forward, only to come to a sudden stop as the man in front of her burst out laughing.

"I am so clumsy. My wife says I fall over my own feet. I am fine, dear. You are new in town. I haven't had the pleasure of meeting you or your family? What's your name, child?"

"Katie, I mean Kathleen O'Callaghan. Sir."

"Nice to meet you, Katie. I am Reverend Timmons. Timothy Timmons. My mother, God rest her, wasn't very original."

Katie stared at the old man with the twinkly eyes. He reminded her of Father Molloy. His smile lit up his eyes, but she couldn't imagine Father Molloy laughing and telling jokes. In the house of God.

"What can I do for you, Katie?"

"I have to get married. On Friday. To a man," Katie burst out. *Oh Lord, why did I have to say that?*

"I assume the man knows he is getting married?" Reverend Timmons laughed, but stopped as the tears filled Katie's eyes.

"Why don't you sit down here, child, and tell me your story."

"My story?" Katie rubbed her eyes impatiently. She didn't know why she was crying.

"We all have a story, and I have a feeling yours is mighty interesting. In fact, if you have time, why don't we go back to the house? Mrs. Timmons was making molasses cookies when I came out this morning. Should be done by now." He patted his stomach. "You would be doing me a favor. She can't tell me off for eating them if I have a guest with me."

Katie nodded, struggling to get her emotions under control. She needed to talk to someone. Ellen was too young. She followed the Reverend into the little house set back from the church. It was small but pretty. The walls had been freshly washed white, she guessed at the same time as the church. She followed the Reverend in the front door, listening as he called out to his wife.

The delicious smell coming from the kitchen caused her stomach to rumble. The Reverend laughed as she blushed.

"Judith, come meet Miss Katie O'Callaghan. I told her you made cookies and she insisted on calling in to try some." He winked at Katie as she put a hand to her mouth, trying not to laugh.

"You old fool. I am not about to fall for that one. No doubt he told you I wouldn't let him have a cookie. Nice to meet you, Katie."

Katie nodded at the older woman. She looked older than her husband, but her eyes sparkled in a similar way. The loving look they exchanged as Mrs. Timmons had teased her husband increased Katie's sense of unease. She wanted her husband to look at her in the same light. Would he?

She dragged her concentration back to Mrs. Timmons, who was still chattering away. "Why don't you take a seat in the parlor? I will bring you in some coffee and cookies. Just for you, mind. Don't let this old chestnut have any."

"Just one, my dearest, you know I can't resist your baking."

Mrs. Timmons laughed her way back toward the kitchen. Katie took a seat in the parlor. It was rather threadbare, and she noted some neat patching on the cushions. There were no religious pictures decorating the walls such as those you would find in a priest's house.

She wondered how many other lost souls had been counseled in this room. Lost souls? Isn't that just what she would become if she didn't get married in her faith in a proper church by a real priest?

"Don't look so frightened, child. I am not going to bite. Why don't you tell me what has you so worried looking? I am a good listener. Kind of goes with the job."

"I am not sure where to begin." Katie looked at her hands. She was sure he wouldn't look too kindly at her if he knew she was here to marry a man she hadn't met. Also, she was catholic. What if he threw her out the door? She looked up and found him staring at her, his eyes a mixture of concern and something else. Pity? She didn't want anyone's pity.

"I find it best to start at the beginning. First, though, please have a cookie and some coffee. Most stories are best told on a full stomach."

Katie took a bite, although the last thing she felt like doing was eating. Her stomach was turning so fast, she felt dizzy. Oh, it was no good. She put the cookie and coffee down and stood up.

"I'm sorry, Reverend, I shouldn't be here. I need to go now."

"Sit down, child. You need to talk to someone. Why not me?"

Years of doing what she was told made her sit down again. She started talking, and once she got going, she didn't stop until the end.

"So there you have it. I am to marry a man who sent for me by post." She waited for the fire and brimstones to start falling, but instead they sat in silence. A full minute passed before she could look at the Reverend. He seemed to be deep in thought. Katie stood.

"I guess you want me to leave now."

"Why would I do that? We have a wedding to plan."

Katie sat. "You mean you will do it? Even though I am not a member of your congregation?"

"Child, I believe that God has sent you to Clover Springs for a reason."

"But you don't think less of me for marrying a man I haven't met?"

"Katie O'Callaghan, you seem a fine young woman. You are doing a great job of looking after your younger sister just as your parents asked of you. You have been honest with me. Perhaps I would prefer you had a chance to meet Mr. Cassidy, maybe even be courting him for a while to make sure this marriage was a good match for both of you, but I have to be realistic. There are few single, decent women in these parts. In fact, there are few women, period. Our men have to resort to certain measures to find brides. I am very glad you came to Clover Springs. I hope you and Mr. Cassidy will be happy and will settle in these parts."

"But I was raised a Catholic."

"That doesn't bother me none. I get the impression you would rather get married than wait for Father Cleary to arrive. He does visit every month or so. But... well, perhaps I best say nothing."

"Father Cleary wouldn't approve of me marrying a stranger." Katie scowled.

"I think it would be more the fact he wouldn't approve of you marrying outside your faith. Father Cleary is a very fair-minded individual, but he is what I would call traditional."

"I don't want to wait any longer than I have to."

'I will perform the service, child. No issue with that, provided you assure me you are happy to proceed." Reverend Timmons looked at her sternly. "I believe marriage is forever, so any doubts you may have should be dealt with before you take your vows."

"I want to be married as soon as possible. No doubt about that." Katie tried to ignore the voice in her head. Lying to a Reverend wasn't as bad as lying to a real priest. Was it?

Reverend Timmons stood up, a smile once more

brightening his face. "I shall see you on Friday at noon. Don't forget to bring your witnesses."

At Katie's blank stare, he laughed. "In order for your marriage to be legal, you must have two witnesses to sign for you. I can bring Mrs. Timmons along. She loves a good wedding. Mrs. Sullivan will also be happy to oblige. The women of Clover Springs are no different than women anywhere else. They love the chance to get all dressed up in their finery.

Katie thanked the kindly couple and walked back to the boarding house, her steps much lighter. Everything was going to work out just fine. Then she noticed the position of the sun. It was nearly lunchtime. Hurrying, she hoped Ellen had stirred the stew.

CHAPTER 26

Katie sat down, glad to take the weight off her feet, but she was too worked up to relax. She looked around, spotting a mending basket stored behind a chair. She went over, lifted it up and decided to help Mrs. Sullivan. Sewing always relaxed her, although mending wasn't her favorite activity. She preferred making things from scratch.

She took out a shirt, it smelt of Daniel. She inhaled deeply, holding the material closer. He was everything she had dreamed of finding in a man. Kind, caring and funny. Handsome, too. She couldn't forget that. She straightened up her needle, ready to sew in some missing buttons. She tried hard to concentrate on her fiancé. But no matter how many ways she tried to dress it up, the fact remained that he had left her and

Ellen to survive alone in a new town. Okay, he didn't know about Ellen, but that made it worse, not better. As far he knew, Katie was alone. He hadn't mentioned money either. Surely he could have found a way to be in Clover Springs quicker? Maybe he had decided against getting married. What would she do then? *I'd be free. I could marry someone I loved.* Katie shook her head. Thinking that way only led to more heartache.

* * *

LATER, Mrs. Sullivan made her way downstairs for a little while, complimenting Ellen and Katie on their hard work. They sat at the table drinking milk.

"The place looks wonderful. I have never seen it so clean." Mrs. Sullivan looked around, her pleasure evident by the way her eyes sparkled.

"Looks good, don't it Ma? And no offense, but the food has been great, too."

"Typical man. Thinking of his stomach." Mrs. Sullivan's tone told them she wasn't annoyed at her son's teasing.

"Katie's getting married on Friday."

Katie almost groaned out loud. What did Ellen have to go and announce that for? She stared at the table, not wanting to look at Daniel's face. She could feel his eyes on her. She took a couple of deep breathes before saying, "Mr. Cassidy sent me a telegram. He will arrive on Friday. I have spoken to Reverend Timmons. He is happy to marry us, but we will need some witnesses. Mrs. Timmons has agreed to be one and I was hoping you would agree to be the other." Katie looked at Mrs. Sullivan, noting the fact that the lady was staring at her son. Katie followed her gaze, but as soon as her eyes met Daniel's, he turned and stalked out of the room. She looked back at the table, her hands twisting in her lap.

"Why can't I be a witness?" Ellen said, seemingly unaware of the currents in the room.

"You are too young, child. I will be happy to be your witness, Katie. Are you sure you want me to be?"

Katie knew by the way Mrs. Sullivan was looking at her that her question asked a lot more. She nodded her head, not trusting her voice to sound normal. She didn't want to upset Ellen any more. The young girl had cried when she first told her about the telegram. She didn't want to leave Clover Springs. If truth be told, neither did Katie.

* * *

DANIEL STOMPED down the main street, a thunderous mask on his face. He barely noticed people as he marched by. Married on Friday. How could she go ahead with getting wed to a man she knew nothing about? *She doesn't know you either.* He kicked at the dust. No woman had got under his skin the way Katie O'Callaghan had. Not only was she physically attractive, but she was good company too. She made him laugh even when her temper was stirring. She was kind and thoughtful. She was also as stubborn as Betsy, the old mule his father had given him when he was a boy. Betsy would kick anyone who came near her. Why did she have to go marry this Cassidy? He needed a wife. Why not marry him instead? He needed a drink. *No, that was the way of fools.* What he needed was some physical labor to tire him out and take his mind off a woman with violet eyes and hair the color of black silk. He headed to the livery. Old George always welcomed a hand with the animals.

Daniel rubbed the horse down, enjoying the comfort the black horse gave him. *I must be loony. Standing here talking to a horse, telling him all about some girl.* Katie wasn't just another girl, though. She was the first woman he had met to make a real impact on him. He found himself racing through the chores to spend time with her. Any excuse and he was back in the house just to see her for a few seconds. *She must think I live under Ma's skirts.*

He'd been brought up properly and therefore,

another man's bride was off limits. But even the knowledge she belonged to someone else didn't stop him behaving like a lovesick puppy. Maybe that banker had been right. It was time for him to find a wife. Katie had come out west as a mail order bride. He should speak to her about how to go about getting someone like her for himself. But he didn't want someone else. He wanted her.

He muttered something, causing old George to stare at him.

"What?"

"Don't be glaring at me, young Sullivan. I'm not the source of your problems. Why don't you go see Davy? He has plenty of work for you to do. Hard labor works best for what ails you, son."

"There's nothing ailing me."

"You keep telling yourself that. We, that horse and myself, know better. I'm not so old that I can't remember the effect of a pretty face. The whole town is talking about the young'uns staying at your ma's house. They be mighty pretty."

"One of them is still a kid. There isn't such a shortage of women that men need to start leering over a child."

"No need to bite my head off. Get yourself out to Davy's, lad, and cool off."

Daniel stamped outside, mounted and took off for

his brother's ranch. Old George was right. Some hard labor would take his mind off his problems and his brother always needed an extra pair of hands. Daniel cheered up somewhat. Mrs. Higgins might even have baked today. His stomach rumbled in anticipation.

CHAPTER 27

Katie was too restless to go to bed. Ellen was fast asleep and she guessed Mrs. Sullivan was, too. She had retired to her room some time ago, leaving Katie to clear up the kitchen. To be fair, Katie had insisted she needed to keep busy rather than dwell on her wedding. If she stopped working, she would start thinking about Mam and Daddy. They wouldn't approve of her plans.

The door banged. He was back. Katie scrubbed the gleaming pot, hoping he wouldn't come into the kitchen.

"Any coffee left, Ma? Oh, it's you."

Katie smarted at the disappointment in his tone.

"Sorry, I didn't think anyone would want some this late. I will make up a fresh batch."

"Why are you doing it?"

“Making fresh coffee? You can make it yourself if you want to.”

“You know that’s not what I meant.”

Katie didn’t dare turn around to look at him. “Mr. Sullivan, it’s not any of your business what I do.”

“No, I guess that’s true. It isn’t. But I can’t understand why a girl like you feels the need to marry a stranger. I need a wife, but that doesn’t mean I am going to send for one by mail.”

“Why?”

“Cause I would have to know whether I like her or not. You can’t tell that from a letter.”

Katie knew she should leave the room, but curiosity got the better of her.

“Why do you have to get married?”

“Oh, that. The banker fella I met with seems to think that cowboys are a poor investment. He reckons I need a wife or I will hightail it off into the sunset.”

Katie laughed at the expression on his face.

“It’s not a laughing matter. If I haven’t got a wife in a month’s time, the bank won’t give me the loan I need to buy the store. Mr. Brook will have to sell to someone else.”

“I can’t see you working in a store.” Katie frowned as he scowled.

“So you are another one who thinks I am just a stupid cowboy?”

"No, not at all. You just look, I mean your body is..." Katie's cheeks heated up. She risked a quick glance at his face to read amusement and something else in his eyes. She got even more flustered. "Oh, it's late and I need to be up early. Please excuse me." *Heavens, he is going to think I am so forward. Mentioning his body. Of all things you could do, Katie O Callaghan.*

"Of course. Don't let me keep you." Daniel stood as she went to leave through the kitchen door.

"Excuse me," she said.

He didn't move, but simply stood looking down at her. She didn't want to look up at him, but her eyes didn't obey. They were locked on his. Once more she felt the connection between them. Her body swayed closer to his, her eyes drawn to his lips. She wondered what it would feel like if he were to kiss her. He took a step closer.

"Katie."

He put his two hands on either side of her face and gently brought his lips down to graze hers. His scent was intoxicating. She wanted to move closer, for his lips to...

Mr. Cassidy. Oh my, what am I doing?

Startled, she pushed him away. She couldn't say anything, but ran through the door. How could she have let herself down like that? An engaged woman kissing another man. Mam would turn in her grave.

* * *

DANIEL STOOD where she had left him. It had felt so right holding her in his arms. Sure, he knew he was attracted to her, but it was more than that. There had been plenty of pretty saloon girls he found attractive. He could still smell her scent. This was different, and not just because of her innocence. That was obvious based on the reaction to his kiss. When she had moved closer, it had taken all his self control not to deepen the kiss. He wondered if she tasted as good as she smelled. He had resisted the urge to mold her body to his, to show her the effect she had on him. He wanted her to respond to his kiss, to open her mouth under his. By God, he had never wanted a woman as much as this one. He couldn't stand by and let her marry another man. *You can't stop her. Nobody not even Ma would agree to you stealing another man's bride.*

* * *

THE NEXT FEW days were difficult. Mrs. Sullivan needed to rest, so Katie and Ellen continued to do her chores around the boarding house. Katie would have been glad of the distraction were it not for the fact that Daniel was still in Clover Springs. She didn't want him in danger, but she found herself praying he would leave with the sheriff soon. It was hard to concentrate on her work when he was around, never mind her forthcoming wedding.

He consumed her thoughts. She could still feel the touch of his lips against hers. Unable to sleep, she wondered what it would have been like if she hadn't stopped his kiss. Closing her eyes, she relived every moment feeling his body against hers, his arms holding her tight. She couldn't bear to be near him, terrified her true feelings would be plain for all to see.

The sheriff had decided it was pointless trying to find the raiders. He had heard from other lawmen that the gang had hit another train, this time killing some passengers. The raiders were assumed to have headed south. The Texas rangers were on their tail and everyone knew it was only a matter of time before they were caught to face punishment for their crimes.

"Ma asked me to chop some more wood. Is there anything else you can think of that needs doing?"

Katie started. She hadn't heard him come into the kitchen. Her hands shook so much, she was thankful she was washing dishes. "The chimney is smoking a lot. Could you have a look at it, please?" At his frown, she swallowed. She couldn't understand why he was angry with her. Didn't he understand she had given her word to Mr. Cassidy. She smiled, trying to make amends. "It doesn't have to be today if you have other chores to do."

He didn't look up but his tone was sharp. "I've got to see Mr. Brook, but I will be back later. Do you need anything from the store?"

She did, but she would go herself later. She didn't want to be more of a burden than he obviously felt she was.

"No, thank you." Katie turned her attention back to the dishes. She started making a list of her chores in her head. Anything to distract her from Daniel. Why can't he hurry up and leave?

She waited, her neck muscles tensing until she heard the door slam behind her. She let out a deep breath allowing a few tears to fall down her cheeks. If only she could have met him before she made her promise.

DANIEL STALKED down the street toward the mercantile. Why couldn't Friday come faster? At least then he wouldn't have to deal with her being in the house day after day. He wouldn't see her smile that lit up the whole room, smell her perfume or have to deal with her sunny nature. He wouldn't get to eat her wonderful cooking either. He kicked at the dust, the scowl on his face enough to stop most of the town folk from giving him their usual greeting.

Ma was on his back, too. Just last night, she had given him another talking to. She wanted to know what was wrong. He couldn't tell her about the banker's conditions on the loan. She had enough to worry about with getting better.

He pushed the store door open so fast, he nearly knocked over Old George. His friend's parcels fell to the ground. "Who's chasing you?"

"Sorry." Daniel grunted as he picked up the packages.

"When you going to get rid of this temper? It don't suit you. Need to find yourself a woman. That will cure what ails you."

George hurried away before Daniel could reply. Mr. Brook stood at the counter, a grin on his face.

"Is it true?"

"What?" Daniel tried to even his tone. He had been brought up not to be rude to his elders.

"So it is true. A young woman has got under your skin. Would it be that lovely Irish girl who came in here the other day? Hair the color of midnight?"

Daniel didn't acknowledge what the storekeeper had said. "What do you want to do today? More stock-taking?" asked Daniel.

"Why don't we start with a coffee first? You know where the kitchen is."

Daniel returned shortly with the coffee. The store was empty.

"Would it help to tell me what's eating you?"

Daniel stirred his coffee. He needed to tell the old man about the banker. It was only fair.

"I don't think I can buy the store."

Mr. Brook looked surprised.

"I thought you wanted the store, Daniel."

"Oh, I do, sir, but the… Well the thing is…"

"Spit it out lad. I haven't got all day. Is it money?"

"Sort of." At Mr. Brook's puzzled expression, Daniel sighed and put the spoon down. He crossed his arms across his chest. "The bank won't lend me the balance of the money I need to buy the store. I don't have enough saved."

"But why, lad? Did you not show them the books I gave ye? It's a great store and the price is fair. Isn't it?"

Daniel wanted the floor to swallow him. "It's not the price or the books, it's me. They don't think I am a good risk."

"What? You are young, healthy and strong. You have saved enough to pay for more than half the store. What else could they want?"

"A wife."

Mr. Brook sputtered on his coffee. "What's a wife got to do with my store?"

"The banker seems to think I won't be able to stay in one place for long. He said I will find the pull of the trail too attractive and will be off chasing steers as soon as I feel like it. I tried to tell him that those days are behind me. I only ever got involved with wrangling to get the money together to buy me a business. I want to stay in Clover Springs. Ma needs me nearby. When you said you were selling the store, it was the opportunity I was looking for. But now I can't buy it." Daniel paused, looking at the man who meant a lot more to his family than just being a neighbor.

"I am sorry, Mr. Brook. I know you depended on my buying the store so you could go live with Jessica back East. I have racked my brains, but there is no way I can find a wife in a month."

"What does your Ma think?"

"I haven't told her yet. With her being poorly, I didn't want to add to her worries. I have tried everything. I asked Davy if he could lend me the rest of the money, but he has been helping Brian out with law school. He doesn't have that type of cash. I thought then I could look for these raiders and earn some of that reward."

"Oh, lad, it's a fine mess we are in, isn't it? But as my old daddy used to say, two heads is better than one. We will find a way to keep those bankers happy. Let's think on it a while. Why don't you go see how your Ma is? Come back tomorrow and we will have another talk."

"Sure thing, Mr. Brook. Thank you for being so nice about it. I wouldn't mess up your plans. I hope you know that."

"Daniel Sullivan, I have known you since you were no more than a glimmer in your father's eye. It's a pity we don't have a bank here in Clover Springs. A local banker is much more easily influenced than a fella sitting in a big office up in Denver."

CHAPTER 28

The morning of her wedding, Katie was up early. Mrs. Sullivan, who had fully recovered, had prepared a bath for her and lent her some scented soap.

"It's not every day a girl gets married. It's such a pity your own kin aren't here to share the day with you."

"It is best. My father wouldn't hold with me marrying someone I haven't met yet. It's different back home. Usually you marry someone you have known all your life. Occasionally you may marry a cousin or distant relative of your neighbor. But marrying someone you have only exchanged letters with..." Katie paused. "He would rather die than give me away today."

"Was it so bad you had to leave Ireland? I thought

the famine was all but over? I can't bear to think of my Elizabeth having to make a journey like the one you and Ellen have endured. She is lucky to have you with her."

"I am the fortunate one. Ellen has a way of making everyone laugh. She sees the sunny side of everything. I am altogether too serious if she is not around. I just hope…" Katie fell silent. It wasn't appropriate for her to discuss her betrothed, even with someone who had the potential of becoming a very dear friend.

"What do you hope, Katie? Do you have to go through with the wedding today? Before you think it's charity I am offering you, I would expect you to work hard. Both of you. You could consider staying with me and courting your husband before you make such a commitment."

"You are so very kind, but no thank you. I have already given Mr. Cassidy my word, and I never break a promise. I hope he won't mind taking Ellen on as well. We are both hard workers and will earn our keep, but I do not want to leave her alone anywhere. She is too young and naive in the ways of the world."

Mrs. Sullivan sighed. "If you are sure, I won't stand in your way. I just wanted you to know you have options."

"I know that, and I am grateful, but as my mother

used to say, I have made my bed and now I must lie in it."

Mrs. Sullivan shook her head before leaving Katie to have her bath in peace.

It didn't take long to walk to the church. Katie struggled to calm her emotions as she stood outside accompanied by Ellen and Mrs. Sullivan. Katie couldn't help but pray Mr. Cassidy would be late, as it would delay her wedding for a little while longer. Now that the time had come to pledge to love, honor and obey a man she hadn't met, she wasn't as sure she could go through with it.

Her eyes searched the town for Daniel. She didn't know if she was upset or relieved there was no sign of him.

"Not what you dreamt of, is it?" Ellen whispered.

Katie couldn't answer; the lump in her throat was too big. Picking up her skirt she walked up the steps. Reverend Timmons was right. The women of Clover Springs did enjoy a wedding. She was surprised to find a small crowd waiting inside the church. It didn't take long for news to spread in this part of the world. She looked at the men wondering if one was Mr. Cassidy. But he would be standing at the altar not sitting in a pew. In his letters, her beau had described himself as being tall, with good looks and plenty of charm. *Just like Daniel.*

Just then, she heard loud voices. A couple of men accompanied Reverend Timmons into the Church. Their appearance left a lot to be desired. They looked expectantly around them.

Katie kept her eyes glued to the floor, hoping neither of these men was her soon-to-be husband.

"I am Virgil Cassidy and this here be my brother, Montis." He spat on the ground before moving toward Katie. "Is this his wife to be? Isn't he a lucky fellow?"

Katie shivered, trying hard to swallow the bile in her throat as Virgil Cassidy looked her up and down. She crossed her arms. It was as if he could see beneath her clothes. She looked to her beau only to find him staring at his shoes. He seemed embarrassed, as if he would prefer to be anywhere but here.

Her stomach quivered and it took every ounce of self-control to speak. Her voice shaking slightly, she stepped forward.

"I am Kathleen O'Callaghan, and this is my sister Ellen. I am pleased to make your acquaintance." Deliberately, Katie ignored Virgil and directed her greeting to her soon-to-be husband. He didn't look up not even when his brother laughed.

"You're a spirited filly. Maybe you are marrying the wrong brother. Perhaps I should stand in his place." Virgil took a step nearer. Katie instinctively stood back, wanting to put as much distance between them as possible.

"Thank you for the offer, but my contract is with Montis Cassidy. He is the one I promised to marry." Katie cursed the fact that her voice shook. She didn't want this man to know just how much he scared her.

"Perhaps I can marry your sister then. We could have a double wedding. Wouldn't that be something?" Virgil made a show of bowing to Ellen as if courting her.

The small congregation heard Katie's intake of breath before she fainted right there in front of everyone. Or at least that's what she hoped they would think. As expected, Mrs. Sullivan ordered everyone to stand back and give her some air. The older woman knelt down beside Katie.

"Katie, are you all right?"

"Sorry, I guess I shouldn't have skipped breakfast, but I was so excited about my wedding day. I am being silly, but I do need some air. Could you please help me out to the step? I can't breathe in here," Katie said in what she hoped was a dramatic tone. When Mrs. Sullivan leaned forward to help her up, she saw Virgil make his way toward his brother. She took the opportunity to whisper to Mrs. Sullivan that they needed to leave now. Her new friend gave her a quizzical look before saying smoothly, “Out of our way, gentlemen. It would seem that the teasing has got a little too much for the bride-to-be. Let her grab a bit of air. You don’t mind waiting, do you, Reverend? Thank you.” She didn’t even give Reverend Timmons a chance to answer. “Ellen, take your sister’s other arm and help me.”

Ellen did as she was bid. Only when they were at the door did Virgil turn to speak.

“Hey, stop, little lady. I was only playing with you. I have me a fiancée already.”

Katie ignored him; she needed to get Mrs. Sullivan and Ellen outside.

“Katie, are you okay? You look like you saw a ghost.”

Katie ignored her sister. She didn’t have much time.

“Mrs. Sullivan, please take Ellen and go get the sheriff and send him here. Then take Ellen back to the boarding house. Do not come back here no matter what happens.”

“The sheriff? Why, Katie?”

“The man in there is one of the train robbers. Please just go and send the sheriff as soon as you can. I will stall them inside for as long as possible. Don’t tell anyone else. We don’t know who was working with him and I want him caught for poor Mr. Smithson.

Hurry, but remember, do not come back no matter what. Promise me."

Ellen dithered, causing Katie to push her sister down the street. She begged Mrs. Sullivan to go after her sister. "I will be fine, Mrs. Sullivan, but please hurry."

Taking a deep breath and rubbing her hands up and down the side of her dress, Katie picked up her skirts and made her way slowly back inside. *Please, God, make them come back soon. Before the ceremony is over.*

CHAPTER 29

The ladies walked as quickly as they could towards the sheriff's office.

"Mrs. Sullivan, stop. I can't breathe," Ellen said, trying to catch her breath.

Mrs. Sullivan didn't slow her pace. "Come on, Ellen. We must hurry. Katie needs us."

Finally, they reached the jailhouse, leaving what seemed like half of Clover Springs staring after them. It wasn't every day the townsfolk saw a matron and a young girl dressed in their Sunday best racing down the street. But there wasn't time to think about that now. Katie was in trouble and needed her help.

Daniel cleared the soiled hay in the livery stables at the end of town, working hard and fast as if the Devil himself was after him. How could she marry a man she had never met? She didn't have to go ahead with the marriage, never mind her talk about giving her word. The pitchfork he was holding hit the bale of hay viciously.

"Hey, take it easy. What that hay ever done to you?"

George, the old stock hand laughed, revealing a wad of half chewed tobacco. At the look on Daniel's face, the laugh quickly turned into a cough. The older man spat a stream of tobacco juice out the side of his mouth, leaving a brown trail on his graying whiskers. "What in blazes has got into you, Sullivan?"

Daniel didn't reply. What was he supposed to say? The woman he loved was getting married to someone else. A stranger nobody in Clover Springs had seen, never mind heard of. *The woman he was in love with.*

What was wrong with him? Standing here up to his neck in evil smelling hay when he should be at the church stopping this farce of a wedding. If Katie knew how he felt, maybe she would change her mind. But she knew already, didn't she?

He went back to pitching the hay once again.

"Steady on, young fella. I haven't done anything, so don't be taking your temper out on the poor hay or me. If you got troubles, you should go sort them out."

Before Daniel could retort, they heard gunshots. His heart froze as he realized they came from the direction of the church. *Katie.* Dropping the pitchfork, he jumped onto his horse and raced off.

Daniel appeared, half dressed, at the church door. Half the town seemed to be there. He grew conscious of the stares. Looking down, he saw his shirt wasn't completely closed and he was in the process of pulling up his suspenders.

His color rose, but still he moved forward. He saw a man he didn't recognize clutching his arm, the blood soaking his shirt. His injury didn't stop the deputy from holding onto him tightly.

The gunshots. Katie? She could be hurt.

KATIE WALKED SLOWLY OUTSIDE, the sunlight blinding her as she struggled to take in what had just happened. Relief flooded through her as she spotted Daniel. *Why wasn't he dressed?*

"Katie, what on earth? Did you get married? I heard gunshots."

"I'm not hurt. I couldn't get married. Oh, Daniel."

"Oh, you feel it too. I wanted to say something but..." He took a step toward her.

Katie clenched her fingers over and over again. She tried but failed to get her shaking limbs under control. A wave of dizziness came over her.

"What?" Was he saying he thought of her too? He couldn't be. Her mind was playing tricks on her. It must be the shock. Anyway, this was neither the time nor the place.

"Daniel, it's him."

"What? Who?"

"One of the men who robbed the train. That's why I asked your mother to go for the sheriff. But he got away."

"Are you telling me you were going to marry a murderer?"

"No. I was going to marry his brother." She didn't want to see the look on his face. She was sure it would mirror the disgust she felt for herself.

"How do you know it was him? They were wearing masks."

"Yes, I know, but one of them had an unusual birthmark on his lower right arm. Today, at the church, he swung his hat forward in his hand and his jacket sleeve rose up, revealing the same birthmark. It's him, I tell you. The one who collected the bags and told Billy they would swing for the robbery. I thought his voice sounded familiar, but I wasn't sure until I saw the mark."

"Did he recognize you?"

Katie shook her head. "I don't think so, but I

delayed the ceremony so long I think he got a little suspicious. He got away in the confusion caused when the sheriff burst in. They have Montis Cassidy, but he's claiming he wasn't involved." She shuddered; she hadn't stopped to consider he might know her, too. What if he came after them? She could have brought trouble right to Daniel's door. Her hand flew to her mouth. Just what had she got the Sullivan's involved in?

"Where is Ma?"

"She went to get the sheriff with Ellen. I assume she took her back to the boarding house. She was wonderful." Katie saw the determined look on Daniel's face. "What are you going to do?"

"I'm going with the sheriff. He will need more men, but first I am taking you back to the boarding house."

Before Katie could say anything, he lifted her on top of his horse before swinging up behind her. Even suffering from shock, her body was fully conscious of his frame. Although he smelled of horses and manure, the temptation to lean closer to him was overwhelming. They were at the boarding house all too quickly. He dismounted before taking her gently in his arms. He held her close for a few minutes. *Did his lips just kiss my hair?* She looked up into his eyes, but his expression was unreadable.

"Stay here. Lock the door behind me and don't open it again until I come back. You promise?"

Katie nodded. She held her hands together in a bid to stop shaking. Now wasn't the time for weakness. She needed to be calm.

"It will be all right." Daniel leant forward to tenderly rub her cheek, his eyes full of concern and something else. He hesitated as if he wanted to say something, but he thought better of it. And then he was gone.

Her face tingled from his touch. Praying for his safety, she walked slowly into the boarding house where she found Mrs. Sullivan trying her best to calm a hysterical Ellen.

* * *

DANIEL PUSHED his horse harder than any of the other men. The sheriff believed the group was heading toward the mountains. They had to get ahead of them before they lost them in the many trails up there. The nerve of the outlaws to come into town. Then again, they probably didn't expect to meet anyone from the train. Good thing Katie recognized one of the men before she went ahead with the wedding. Maybe she still intended to marry the man if he turned out to be telling the truth and wasn't part of his brother's gang.

Anger flooded Daniel. How could he be innocent? Even if he was, he wasn't the man for Katie. She was his. His whole body tightened with the need to get on with the job in hand so he could return to Clover Springs and claim Katie as *his* bride. *His* wife.

CHAPTER 30

On Sunday, Mrs. Sullivan insisted Katie accompany her family to service and afterwards to Davy's ranch for supper. Reverend Timmons spoke for some time, although Katie had to admit he could have been speaking Dutch for all the notice she took. She was too busy worrying about whether the townspeople knew about her or not.

She was relieved Mrs. Sullivan didn't wait to socialize with the other churchgoers, but excused herself, saying loudly that Davy was waiting for them back at his ranch. They took the buggy with Mrs. Sullivan driving. Ellen chatted as they drove out to the ranch, but Katie stayed silent. She pretended she was engrossed in the passing scenery.

Katie looked around her as they drew up to the house. The ranch seemed to go on forever. It would take a few days to cover the entire area on horseback. Her attention shifted back to the house. Mrs. Sullivan had told her stories about coming to Colorado all those years ago. It had been more difficult then. A lot fewer settlers than today, but the neighbors had been kind and helped them settle in. The local Indians had been friendly, too. At least until the Army started forcing them into reservations. Katie had wept at the stories of the massacres that took place in Sand Creek. She was furious that Colonel Chivington hadn't been called to account for his actions.

There was prejudice the world over. No matter where you travelled, there always seemed to be one group of people who were victimized by others simply for their race, color or religious beliefs.

Mrs. Sullivan smiled at Katie, but her eyes were concerned. "Are you feeling all right? You aren't poorly, are you? I knew you worked too hard when I was ill."

Katie shook her head. "I am fine, thank you. I was just thinking of all the stories you told me about this place. It's beautiful. I love the house. It looks like something you would see in a picture."

"It's homey all right, but it lacks a woman's touch. You will see what I mean when you go inside. Mrs. Higgins is a saint living out here amongst all these men. I keep telling Davy that he needs to find a wife.

He needs company. Being alone is not good for any man, but my Davy is sensitive. I want more grandchildren, too, and Mrs. Higgins could do with some help. At her age, it is too much to cope with, but don't tell her I said that. At least not until she's given me the pies she always bakes for us when we visit. I want to eat them, not wear them."

Katie laughed. Mrs. Sullivan was very entertaining. She was fond of the woman beside her and dreaded leaving her.

"Hi, Ma, how are you feeling?" Davy didn't hide his concern too well.

"I'm fine, Davy, don't start fussing. I have had enough of that from Elizabeth and Daniel. This is Katie and Ellen O'Callaghan. They are from Galway, but had lived in Boston for about a year before deciding to come west." Mrs. Sullivan stepped down from the buggy with her son's assistance and headed toward the house. Davy waited to help Ellen and Katie.

"Pleased to meet you ladies." A smile creased his face, but he still looked tired. He explained he hadn't made it into town for Sunday Service due to a cow calving. "It was a bit tricky, but we got there in the end."

"Oh, can I go see her? I love newborns." Ellen clapped her hands in excitement.

"Sure thing, Miss Ellen. Just let me show your sister into the house, unless she wants to come, too."

Katie smiled as she shook her head. "You two go ahead. I will follow Mrs. Sullivan in."

Katie stood and watched as Davy and Ellen headed toward the barn, chatting away. Davy had a nice face. She immediately felt she could trust him. He wasn't as good looking as Daniel, but you could see the family resemblance. Daniel. Where was he now? She hoped he was safe.

She walked into the house. Hearing the ladies talking, she followed their voices into the kitchen just in time to hear Mrs. Higgins comment on how worried Mrs. Sullivan must be.

"I am really sorry. It's all my fault. If I hadn't come to Clover Springs, none of this would have happened."

Mrs. Sullivan took Katie in her arms and gave her a hug. "Stop saying it's your fault. You didn't do anything. Those men are evil and our men have to stand up to them. Clover Springs is a nice place to live and we want it to stay that way. Daniel will be fine. His Pa trained him how to shoot when he was little. He can hold his own. Now let's have a coffee before Elizabeth arrives. Then we can all sit down to dinner. Mrs. Higgins here is an amazing cook. A full stomach will help us all feel better."

"You did well, girl, looking after Martha. I keep

telling her she needs more help in that boarding house, but she don't listen to me. Nobody listens."

"We do listen. I hope to persuade Katie and her sister to live with me. Katie can get work as a seamstress. You should see what she can do with a needle. Ellen can go to school and help me with some chores. It will be perfect for everyone."

Mrs. Higgins stopped stirring the pot to stare at Mrs. Sullivan. "Are you matchmaking again, Martha? Who's the lucky man this time?"

Katie watched the redness spread up from Mrs. Sullivan's neck over her face. "I might think that two young people are a good match, but I won't interfere. I am not that type of mother."

Mrs. Higgins obviously didn't agree if the humph of her reply was anything to go by.

Katie busied herself by looking around the large kitchen. She didn't want to think about romantic involvements. Friday's disaster was too painful and now Daniel was goodness knows where.

Davy and Ellen came in, her younger sister full of delight over the young calves. Not long afterwards, Elizabeth arrived with her family. Dinner took place in the dining room around a big table that could have sat another ten people comfortably. The conversation flowed. The family had lots to catch up on. Mrs.

Sullivan gave them a brief outline of the events that had happened on Friday.

"So Daniel is off with the sheriff? Do they know where the varmints were headed?" Davy asked his Ma as he handed her the serving dish full of potatoes.

"No, but Sandy Scott was with them. If he can't pick up their trail, nobody can." Mrs. Sullivan turned to Katie. "Sandy is part Indian and used to scout for the army. He is getting on a bit now, but there's still no one better at picking up a trail."

Katie nodded, keeping her eyes on her plate. She didn't want to look up and see censure in the faces of Daniel's siblings. Mrs. Sullivan may not blame her, but that didn't mean Davy and Elizabeth would agree.

"How did you come to be a mail order bride, Miss O'Callaghan?" Elizabeth asked just as Katie took a bite of the roast beef. She chewed quickly not wanting to answer with her mouth full.

"I answered an ad I saw in Boston. We were staying with family and it was best I make my own way."

"What Katie means is our uncle and aunt were horrid. I don't ever want to go back to Boston. They were really mean to us."

"Ellen, shush."

"Sounds like the child was just speaking the truth. I've heard jobs are hard to come by in Boston."

"That's true, Mr. Sullivan. There are so many immigrants and not enough positions."

"So what are your plans now? Are you going to stay in Clover Springs?"

Katie crossed her fingers under the tablecloth. "I hope so. Your mother thinks I may be able to secure enough work. I'm a seamstress. Ellen would be able to return to school."

"Aw, I want to keep working. I hate school."

"I think you could do both, little lady, couldn't you? Go to school and then do chores when you come home. My mother could sure use some help."

Katie hid a smile at the look of adoration her sister gave Davy. He had certainly won her heart.

"That's a fine idea, Davy. Thank you"

Katie coughed. It was exactly the same idea she and Mrs. Sullivan had tried to get Ellen to accept and now here she was pretending it was the first she heard of it. *Ellen O'Callaghan, I will have to keep an eye on you. Sure you will be breaking hearts in no time.*

After dinner, Davy showed Ellen and Katie around the ranch. Katie loved the horses. Davy showed her how to gain their trust. They met a couple of the ranch hands, but didn't stop to chat. There was work to be done and they were short-handed due to a couple of them having gone with the sheriff.

"How long do you think they will be gone, Mr. Sullivan?"

"A couple of days or so, I would think. Someone said the Texas Rangers were coming. I guess the sheriff will prefer the non-lawmen get back to their families. It's a busy time of year and most are behind with their chores. The weather was against us for so long, although it seems to have settled this past week."

"You have a beautiful place out here. You can see the sky for miles. I missed that when we were in Boston."

"Did you live out in the prairies in Ireland?"

Katie laughed, but then tried to smother it. She didn't want him thinking she was making fun of him, but the whole of Ireland would probably fit into this prairie. She had found that Americans seemed to forget Ireland was a tiny place. "We lived on a small farm, but the nearest city was about two days' walk away. We had clear skies like these, although it was often raining."

"Could do with more rain over here. The crops need it, but then I guess we are never thankful for what we got. I always seem to be asking for more than giving thanks for what I have. Maybe Ma is right. I should give more attention to going to church."

"Mrs. Sullivan means well. She knows you have a lot of work to do. She is quite concerned about you being here alone." Katie went bright red. How could she have betrayed Mrs. Sullivan's confidence like that? "What I mean is..."

"Oh, don't worry none. Ma isn't very discrete. She tells everyone who will listen I need a wife. She thinks it's time I moved on. Happens she is right. It's been a long time since Tilly... Sorry, Miss O'Callaghan, we best collect Ellen and get back to the others. They will be wondering where we are."

Katie followed Davy in silence. She sensed he needed time to regain his composure. The poor man. She wondered who Tilly was. Mrs. Sullivan hadn't mentioned her.

CHAPTER 31

Monday morning, Katie slipped out of the boarding house intent on going to the mercantile. She wanted to see if Mr. Brook would be interested in employing her. She thanked God she knew how to sew. She had to repay Mr. Cassidy. The thought of keeping any of his blood stained funds was too abhorrent.

She was so lost in thought, she nearly walked past the mercantile, but Mr. Brook happened to come out just at that moment.

"Why, hello again, Miss. Come to drop some more pennies?" He teased her, smiling. Katie tried to smile back, but her face was too tight. His smile turned to a questioning look as he stood holding the door open. Katie nodded and went inside, trying to find her voice.

If she didn't say something soon, she would lose her nerve about asking for a job.

"I would have thought you would have been long gone by now."

Katie's nerve crumbled as she looked into the spiteful face of Mrs. Grey. Why did she have to bump into her?

"I have no idea what you are talking about. Please excuse me." Katie did her best to walk past the other woman, but Mrs. Grey moved in front of her, blocking Katie's escape.

"I think it's a big coincidence that you were on that train. You know the one that was robbed by your in-laws."

"They are not my in-laws," Katie protested, but Mrs. Grey continued nonetheless.

"I wonder if the sheriff is aware. Perhaps someone ought to enlighten him."

Katie saw the redness descend, but even if she had wanted to curb her tongue, it was too late. "Listen to me, Mrs. Grey, I didn't have anything to do with the train robbery. I was a victim just like all the other passengers."

"Humph. I think you will find most people will believe my version of events, young lady. We don't need your sort here in Clover Springs." Katie took a step back as the other woman came closer. She looked around the store for an alternative escape route.

"Begging your pardon, Mrs. Grey, but I believe you are mistaken. I think Miss O'Callaghan and her sister are a welcome addition to this town. We don't have enough real ladies here."

Mr. Brook talked as he walked over and stood between the two women, sheltering Katie behind him.

"Well of all the things to say, Mr. Brook." Mrs. Grey huffed and puffed so much, Katie had to turn her head to hide the giggle wanting to escape. She turned back in time to watch Mr. Brook stride over to the store door, holding it open for Mrs. Grey as she stalked out of the shop.

"That old biddy is one person I won't be missing," Mr. Brook said, winking at Katie.

"Thank you very much for your kind words, Mr. Brook. I am sure Mrs. Grey is only putting into words what other people will be thinking."

Mr. Brook stood silent for a couple of seconds as if he was trying to think of something to say. "I guess you are partly correct. There will be some who will believe anything and everything Mrs. Grey has to say. She could tell them the next shower would be full of gold and they would have their buckets ready to catch it."

Katie laughed at the image, and then fell silent. It

wasn't really a laughing matter. All she had was her reputation, and that was currently in shreds.

"Thankfully, there are good folk in Clover Springs who will dismiss Mrs. Grey's stories as gossip. They will wait to make your acquaintance before making up their minds. I am sure they will find you just as charming as I do. It isn't fair what happened to you, child, but I rather sense that you are used to life being unfair. You can handle the gossip. We have seen evidence of that today. Now, would you join me in a coffee? My throat is awful parched."

Before Katie could decline, he continued. "Then you can tell me what brought you to see me."

Katie enjoyed the coffee and slice of cake Mr. Brook insisted she have. It salved her soul, especially after the trauma of Friday. They discussed the market for her sewing and agreed on a more than generous percentage. Katie would give Mr. Brook 10% of the profits. She had offered more, but as he had pointed out, she would help sales by using materials from the store. He had shown her a work area she could use and had even uncovered an old and rather dusty sewing basket his wife had used. On impulse, Katie had kissed the old man on the cheek when she was leaving. He blushed in response.

"I'm sorry, Mr. Brook, that was forward of me. I forgot myself due to your kindness," Katie said, stammering. "Mam would kill me for forgetting my manners."

"Mrs. Sullivan told me how you looked after her when she fell ill. Not only that, but you looked after her guests as well. You are a fine woman. You would make any man proud, Katie O'Callaghan. If I had a son, I would have wanted him to marry a girl just like you. Now think of what I said about visiting the jailhouse. The sooner you close that door, the quicker you can move on with the rest of what I hope will be a long and happy life."

"I'll go there later. I have to go back to Mrs. Sullivan and tell her my news. She was the one who suggested I come see you. Thank you again, Mr. Brook. See you in the morning."

Katie almost sang as she walked back toward Mrs. Sullivan's house. Even if she only succeeded in attracting half of the demand Mr. Brook anticipated for her dressmaking service, she would soon have sufficient monies to repay Mr. Cassidy. *Maybe I could earn enough to stay here in Clover Springs. Ellen could go to school. We would be free. But would an unmarried girl be allowed to live alone in this town?* Mrs. Grey would not be in favor. Mrs. Grey could take a long walk off a short plank. She was fed up with other people telling her how to live her life. Mr. Brook was right. It was time to make a stand and show the world who Katie O'Callaghan really was.

First, though, she had to get rid of her groom-to-be. Once and for all. With a mutinous look on her face, Katie turned so quickly, the cowboy walking behind her almost plowed into her. Mumbling a quick apology, Katie walked off in the direction of the jailhouse.

She had just crossed the street when she saw Mrs. Grey talking to a friend. The two women were coming straight toward her. There was nowhere to hide, so she best start as she meant to go on. Walking straighter, she continued forward, praying they wouldn't notice her shaking. Before she could greet them, the two women walked straight past her as if she didn't exist. She heard Mrs. Grey say, "Of course, no decent woman," as she walked by but she missed the end of the sentence. Probably a good job, she thought grimly, flexing her fingers and hoping her heart didn't beat loud enough for the whole street to hear. After everything she had been through to get as far as Clover Springs, why did it all have to go wrong now? Mrs. Gantley had arranged dozens of happy marriages for mail order brides. Why did hers have to be a disaster? Despite her best efforts, a tear slipped down her cheek closely followed by a second and a third. Tempted as she was to run back to the boarding house, Katie knew she had to face him.

CHAPTER 32

"Deputy, I don't got no clue about any train robberies. You got to believe me."

"I haven't got to believe nobody. The proof is right there. Your brother was recognized by some of the people he robbed. Or are you going to tell me those good people are seeing things?"

"That's my brother. Not me. I didn't do anything. I haven't been near any train, never mind robbing one. I was home on the ranch the whole time." Montis stopped talking. He didn't like the look on the deputy's face. What had he said?

"Speaking of a ranch, where did you think the money came from for the land and all those animals? Your bride-to-be said you wrote her about having a herd of cattle and some horses. How did you pay for them?"

Montis cursed silently. He was going to kill Virgil if he got to him before the law did.

"Cat got your tongue now, boy? I asked you a question."

"Virgil paid for it." Montis spat out the words, cursing silently. He wasn't taking any heat for Virgil. Not anymore.

As the lawman grinned triumphantly, the sweat ran down Montis's face and arms. "You got to believe me. I'm not a train robber and I never killed no one. I wanted to, sure, but that don't count."

"I reckon you should keep quiet now and take some time to think about what you are going to say to the Judge. Maybe he will just hand you over to the Texas rangers. Heard they were after your gang real bad."

Montis took a gulp of air, feeling lightheaded. Texas rangers? What had Virgil done in Texas? They hung you quicker than they lit a smoke down there. He gripped the bars tighter, thinking he best listen to the deputy.

"Whether you are guilty or not, the fact is your brother and his gang killed a man. A good man who was a favorite of many people around here. Folk aren't going to take too kindly to that, and, well, Virgil isn't here, then…"

The deputy let the silence speak for itself as he left the room.

Montis glared as the lawman left him standing in the cell, dwelling on his misfortune. Why did he come to Clover Springs? Virgil wanted a bride, not him. He should have stayed at home. Least there he couldn't have got into trouble. Home? He didn't have a home now. The sheriff as good as said the land and the animals would be seized. If Friday hadn't been bad enough, this day was just getting worse and worse.

A while later the deputy walked toward Montis. "You got a visitor. Don't make no sense why a real pretty lady would be wanting to see a no account like you."

A pretty lady. He didn't know any ladies, never mind pretty ones. Montis stood up.

"You behave yourself now. The lady be upset enough."

Montis nodded, still not quite following. He looked at the door, sucking in his breath as a beautiful girl walked in. It was her. The girl he was supposed to wed on Friday. What on earth did she want? Surely she wasn't expecting the wedding to go ahead. With Virgil on the run and himself locked up, he didn't need any more problems. He was about to tell her to go away when he noticed she looked like she'd been crying. His stomach dipped. He wasn't used to women and mightn't like them much, but that didn't mean he wanted them to cry.

"I am sorry about Friday." Montis spoke, surprising both of them.

The girl behaved as if he hadn't said anything. She walked over to the cell.

"I came by to give you this. It is all I have. I will have to send the rest of the money to you." Katie held out a small bag of coins.

"I don't want your money. You keep it." Montis took a step back.

"I don't want anything from you, especially money that has blood on it."

"Blood? Ah, now don't tell me you believe I am guilty, too. I regret what my brother done, but he is not me."

She didn't even look at him while he was talking. For some reason, her attitude got through to him worse than the threats from the lawman. He wasn't respectable. Sure, he hadn't gone on any raids with Virgil, but he hadn't asked any questions either. He had been happy to enjoy whatever Virgil had provided and never once questioned him about where the cash came from. *You didn't ask, as you didn't want to know the answer. You know Virgil. He isn't the type to get too upset about hurting other folk.*

Montis felt his legs give way. He was guilty, too.

He hadn't done anything. Because of him, this girl had travelled across the country away from her family. He had a duty to her regardless of what he wanted.

"Listen, Miss, I promise on the Good Book I didn't have anything to do with the train robberies or any of the other things that gang was involved in. I haven't got much. The ranch, animals and everything else I wrote you about belongs to Virgil."

The deputy's cough reminded Montis they weren't alone.

"What I mean to say is that you came all this way to wed me and if you were willing to proceed, we could ask the deputy to get the preacher over here. Then you wouldn't be alone in this wild country. We still got a contract. What do you say?"

He looked into her violet eyes, growing larger as she digested what he had said.

"She is not alone, Mr. Cassidy." Montis had been so intent on staring at Katie, he hadn't noticed the older woman coming into the jail. With her arrival, Katie's face lost much of her pinched look. Montis watched helpless as the lady put her arm around Katie's shoulders drawing the younger girl closer to her. "She is coming home with me. I took the liberty of speaking to the Judge. As your future is somewhat uncertain, it wouldn't be in anyone's interests to try to enforce the contract. She is, as are you, free to marry someone else."

"But what if I want—"

"What you want, Mr. Cassidy, is of no concern of mine. I am sure Miss O'Callaghan feels the same. Decent folk do not converse with criminals. While you may not have been involved with your brother's gang, you enjoyed the fruits of his murderous activity. That makes you as guilty as he is."

The older woman took hold of the younger girl's hand and pulled her into an embrace. Gently pushing back tendrils of jet-black hair, Montis heard the matron whisper, "Come along home now, Katie. The last few days have taken their toll. Mr. Brook told me what happened at the store. You need looking after. Let me be your friend and look after you, just as you looked after me when I was ill. Ellen is waiting for you back at my house."

Montis was tempted to say something, but really, what could he say? Whether he liked it or not, he had known Virgil was up to something and he didn't have the guts to face him. He walked over to the small cot and sat down, putting his head in his hands. To think he had thought getting married was the worst thing that could happen to him.

. . .

MARTHA SULLIVAN PULLED the door behind her before adjusting her bonnet. Taking Katie's arm, she guided her down the boardwalk towards the boarding house.

"Thank you, Mrs. Sullivan. How did you know where to find me?"

"I haven't known you long, Katie, but I believe you are honest and hardworking. It didn't take long to work out where you would go when Ellen said you had gone to the store. I checked with Mr. Brook, and he told me something of your conversation. Out of concern. We have known each other for a long time. Mr. Brook is not one for gossip."

Katie half listened to Mrs. Sullivan, but her thoughts were overwhelming. She had to put them into words.

"He was going to be my husband. I felt, oh, I don't know."

"You don't owe that man anything. As my mother used to say, show me your friends and I will tell you what you are like. He may not be guilty of the same crimes as his brother, but the fact remains he lived off the proceeds of a life of crime. Even if he is not convicted, he will lose everything. You do not deserve that, Katie, love. You haven't done anything."

"I promised to marry a man I had never met." Katie swallowed a sob. "I am being punished for my sins."

"Nonsense. My God doesn't believe in that sort of

payback. You ask Reverend Timmons. You made a decision based on the circumstances you were in. You could have found other ways to earn a living. There are plenty of saloon owners who would have employed you." Katie shuddered, causing Mrs. Sullivan to pull her closer. "You did what you had to, love, and nobody is going to judge you for that. Now let's get home and get you warmed up. You are chilled to the bone."

Katie embraced Mrs. Sullivan while sending a silent prayer of thanks to her Mam. Surely she had intervened. If the sheriff hadn't arrived, she would be married now and could have spent her wedding night in a cell. Shivering and not from the cold, Katie edged even closer to Mrs. Sullivan and allowed the older woman to steer her toward the boarding house. She hoped they wouldn't meet anyone else on the way back.

CHAPTER 33

Daniel observed Katie, secure in the knowledge the darkness hid his presence. Ma had told him she had been to the jailhouse and officially ended things. He clenched his knuckles as he thought again how close he had come to losing her. If she hadn't been so brave, she would be married to that varmint and now going through goodness knows what. No woman deserved a life like that, never mind his Katie.

She was beautiful. No, that wasn't the right word. She was more than that. Some of her hair had escaped its braid and flowed down her back, the deep shine reflecting in the moonlight. He ached to touch it, wondering if it felt as soft as it looked. Her shoulders shook as loud shuddering sobs wracked her body. He plunged his hands into his pockets in an effort to stop himself from reaching out to her. She needed time to grieve and wouldn't thank him for embarrassing her. Her whole future had fallen apart and that was scary enough for a guy, let alone a young girl like her. Girl? Who was he kidding? She was all woman. He waited a few minutes, trying to find the right words. He didn't want her to leave. Yet how could he convince her to stay?

"Katie, it's Daniel. I just wanted to check and see you were okay?" She didn't turn, but he saw her shake her head.

"Leave me be, please. I need to be alone."

Her despairing sob tore at his heart. He took two steps toward her, turning her gently to face him. She glimpsed up at him for a second before looking back at the floor. He took her chin in his hand, forcing her to face him. Pushing her hair back, he caressed her cheek. Her skin was so soft against his calloused hands. She stiffened and tried to move out of his embrace, but he held on.

"Don't cry. I can't bear to see you this unhappy."

She stared up at him, shock written all over her face. Her gaze flitted to his mouth, her thoughts making her cheeks turn crimson. She looked away, but it was too late. He had seen the desire flare in her eyes and the hope he had tried to bury burned brightly. She had feelings for him. He knew it.

Slowly, he bent his head toward hers. Caressing her mouth with his own, he closed his eyes as his arms tightened around her body. He fought the desire to crush her to him, instead drawing her gently closer. He didn't want to frighten her off. She was so innocent. Again she stiffened momentarily, but he plunged on. He had to show her how much she meant to him. He couldn't let her leave. Not now.

A weak sigh escaped her lips as she melted into his embrace. With a heavy groan, he wrapped his fingers in her loose hair. It was so soft and smelt like roses. The taste of her lips under his was better than he had ever imagined. He could kiss her forever and never get tired. Desire lurched through him as her mouth opened and she returned his kiss. She clung to him, intensifying his feelings. Oh, how he wanted her. Their kiss lasted several seconds, their bodies molded as closely as their clothes allowed.

A door banged, bringing him back to the present as effectively as a bucket of ice water. What if they were seen like this? Katie's reputation, what was left of it, would never recover. He couldn't let that happen.

Katie was so relaxed in his arms, it was obvious she hadn't heard the door. Reluctantly, he broke their kiss and pushed her gently away. He struggled to get his breathing under control. He couldn't look at her, his shame overwhelming. He had treated his Katie like a woman from the saloon.

He stiffened, shoving his hands in his pockets.

"Katie, um, I mean Miss O'Callaghan, I apologize. I shouldn't have behaved like that. Will you please forgive me?"

KATIE STARED AT HIM, trying to get a hold of her feelings. How could he kiss her so deeply one minute and then thrust her away so sharply the next? Her heart beat so fast she was sure it would spring from her chest any second. Forgive him? For treating her like a shameless hussy? *You enjoyed it.* Her body tingled from his touch and truth be told, she didn't know how hard she could fight if he decided to take her in his arms once more. Maybe that woman had been right. She was a shameless vixen - traveling all this way to marry a man she hadn't met and now behaving like this. Anger competed with desire. *How dare he treat her like this? How dare he stop that delicious kiss?* A true lady would slap a man across the face for less than what he had done this evening. But she wasn't a lady, was she? She had behaved wantonly and it was his entire fault.

Scarcely realizing what she was doing, she lifted her palm and smacked him straight across the cheek.

"How dare you?" She hissed as she stormed back into the house, praying fervently she wouldn't meet anyone. One glance at her disheveled state would be enough to prove the truth of the horrible remarks Mrs. Grey had made this afternoon. Holding her hand to her mouth, she ran for her room and shut the door gratefully behind her. Ellen's facial expression when Katie barged into the room proved she had been right to worry.

"What on earth happened to you? Your hair is all over the place and your mouth looks all bruised. You've been crying. Oh, Katie. Did someone hurt you?"

"Hush up, Ellen. Someone will hear you. I'm fine. Go to sleep." Guilt overwhelmed Katie at the look her sister threw her before she turned over to sleep. Katie knew she deserved her reproach for her sharp tone, but she didn't have time to consider her sibling's feelings now. Not when her own were all over the place.

She scrubbed her face raw, trying to remove all traces of the kiss. It wasn't possible, not when every delicious second was seared into her memory. *Katie O'Callaghan, just what have you done now?*

. . .

DANIEL PACED THE ROOM. He felt like one of the wild horses suddenly confined to a holding pen. What had he been thinking of, treating a virtuous woman like that? He could only hope that she would forgive him in the morning. She had enjoyed it, too. The response of her body told him so, despite her protest. He touched his cheek gingerly. For someone who looked like she would blow over in a strong wind, she had a powerful right hook.

Remorse flooded through him as he remembered the look of pure fear on her face as she raced away from him. He wanted to go to her now, pull her into his arms and reassure her she would never be alone again. He strode up the stairs and stopped outside her door. He listened carefully, but he couldn't hear a sound. He couldn't knock and disturb her at this time of night. It wasn't proper, and even if it had of been, she shared a room with her sister. He wasn't going to be responsible for frightening someone else tonight. Swallowing a curse, he gave one last look at the closed door before marching off back down the stairs. He best go to bed before he caused any more trouble.

KATIE HELD HER BREATH, convinced she had heard someone standing outside their bedroom door. Ellen's gentle snores filled the room, but some instinct told her Daniel was just outside. She stared at the door, part of her willing him to come in, but the more sensible part willed him to leave. She didn't completely understand what had happened earlier, but she knew enough to believe herself lost if he attempted to kiss her again.

CHAPTER 34

"Good morning, Mrs. Sullivan. Isn't that a shocking turn of events at the church? I do hope you are all right. I am sure you felt it was your God given duty to provide a roof to those two girls. Although, I fear your charity may have been misplaced. Clover Springs doesn't need the likes of them stopping by. Hopefully they will leave our little town as soon as the next train arrives."

"Hello, Mrs. Grey. Why thank you for your consideration of my health." Martha Sullivan struggled to make her voice friendly. Truth be told, Mrs. Grey was the last person Mrs. Sullivan wanted to meet today. That woman had a nose for gossip and always turned up when she was least wanted. She had to be careful though as she eyed the woman dressed, as usual, in her best finery. She couldn't afford to make any enemies, especially one as formidable as this. Mr. Grey owned half the town and his wife seemed to believe this gave her permission to treat everyone else badly. Being so wealthy, she could do what she liked in town and nobody would say anything to stop her. Martha didn't like bullies, not even when they were dressed in the guise of respectable old ladies. "I am enjoying having the O'Callaghan sisters as guests. They are welcome to stay as long as they like, although I fear you are right. They may just leave on the next train. There aren't many opportunities for single girls in Clover Springs. Ellen could help teach the younger children if the Reverend goes ahead with his plan for the new school, but Katie would need to pay her way." Martha took a deep breath. She didn't like to ask for favors, but this was for those dear girls. Lord knows they needed as much help as she could give them. "I don't suppose you have heard yet, but Katie is an excellent seamstress. Mr. Brook has kindly allowed her to use his premises. She will have a desk over in that corner and will be available for all sorts of sewing work from mending to making new dresses. Please tell your friends. Katie is a hard worker with plenty of experience."

"I wouldn't be recommending that … that girl to any of my friends. If you ask me, she should be working in the…" Mrs. Grey looked around her before dropping her tone to a conspiratorial whisper, "saloon, not trying to pass herself off as a respectable woman. What type of lady sells herself in marriage to a man she has never met?"

"Mrs. Grey!" Martha was so shocked, she didn't make an effort to control her tone.

"Don't use that tone with me, Mrs. Sullivan. You and I both know that Montis Cassidy sent that girl money and a train ticket to come out to these parts in order to get married. He as good as bought her. She, the little heathen, saw fit to drag her innocent sister with her. Although given she shares parentage, perhaps she was hoping for a similar arrangement with the nearest available man."

"Mrs. Grey, Ellen is barely more than a child and not of an age to get married. Please tell me that is not what you believe. I think Miss O'Callaghan showed true strength of character. She doesn't have a family to take care of her and this was the only way she felt she could look after herself and her sister. Doesn't every woman have the right to her own home, a husband, and, with God's love, a family?"

"God didn't mean for you to enter into a marriage contract with a stranger, least of all a murderer."

"Now that is totally unfair. It wasn't Miss O'Callaghan's intended who murdered poor Mr. Smithson, but his brother's gang. He is hardly responsible, and even if he was, Miss O'Callaghan is completely innocent."

"You can believe what you like, Mrs. Sullivan, but let me tell you that these Irish immigrants are not to be trusted. They are all liars and cheats. Every last one of them."

Martha Sullivan clenched her fists. She wanted nothing better than to take Mrs. Grey by her fur lined collar and throw her out the store door, but that wouldn't be seemly or fitting for a grown woman in her 40s.

Taking a deep breath, Mrs. Sullivan counted to ten before saying sweetly, "Mrs. Grey, let me remind you that my dear departed father-in-law, and founder of this town, was an Irish immigrant."

She had the satisfaction of seeing Mrs. Grey go pale.

"Well, of course I didn't mean..."

"I know exactly what you meant, Mrs. Grey. Now please excuse me. I have chores to attend to. Good day."

Martha Sullivan didn't wait for a response but strode out of the store. She didn't trust herself not to rise to the bait should Mrs. Grey wish to impart any more of her opinions. She was only thankful that the girls hadn't overheard what had been said. They had suffered enough already.

. . .

Katie held herself close against the wall of the store, hoping that the ladies wouldn't come looking at the cloth. She had come in hoping to speak some more to Mr. Brook about how to advertise her new services. She had dipped behind a couple of bales when she saw Mrs. Grey enter the store. She didn't want to speak to anyone right now, especially not someone who had been so unfriendly since her arrival. She hadn't understood what she had done to upset the old woman, but now she knew. Mrs. Grey didn't like her because she was Irish. Katie couldn't do anything about that, but it didn't stop her feeling worse.

Her heart sang as she listened to Mrs. Sullivan defend her honor. At least someone thought good of her. The smile slid from her face. Mrs. Sullivan may have defended her to Mrs. Grey, but how would she feel if she knew Daniel had kissed her? Being his mother, she would think Katie had led him astray.

She considered what the older woman had said about her being a mail order bride. Is that what the other townspeople believed? That she was no better than a common … Katie couldn't bring herself to finish that thought. It was enough she had ruined her own life. A girl's reputation meant everything. She had promised Daddy she would look after Ellen. She'd failed. Not only had she destroyed the O'Callaghan name but she'd nearly got her sister killed in the process. She may not be able to save herself, but she was darn well sure her little sister wasn't going to suffer as a result of her impulsiveness.

She would find a way to get her sister home. Back to their father. He would keep her safe.

CHAPTER 35

Daniel paced up and down the room.

"Why don't you just ask her to marry you and be done with it?" his mother said, smiling as his eyes widened and he came to a sudden halt.

"How did you know?"

"Daniel, you're my son. A poor mother I'd be if I didn't recognize when my son was in love. She is a fine girl. I approve. Now what are you waiting for?"

"It don't seem right. She was going to marry …"

"That was a mistake and we both know it. I think it was God's way to bring Katie and Ellen to Clover Springs. You need a wife and she needs a husband. Even better the two of you have feelings for one another. It's wonderful." Mrs. Sullivan beamed.

Daniel scratched his head. Could he ask her? What would she say?

"Stop hanging about here and go and ask her. Before she gets a chance to make any more plans. She has just come in. I think you will find her in the dining room setting the table."

Mrs. Sullivan walked away, leaving Daniel staring after her. He took a deep breath and walked into the dining room. Katie was there, but she looked as if she had been crying.

"Katie, what is it? You look upset."

Katie impatiently brushed away her tears. "'Tis nothing. I got something in my eye." Katie stared down at the table. The silence grew awkward. "I didn't get a chance to ask you. Did you catch them?"

Daniel shook his head. "We were sent home. The Texas rangers have taken over the search. They didn't want those with no experience ruining their chance of catching those varmints." Daniel swallowed hard. "Katie, could I speak to you?"

"That's what we are doing now, isn't it?" she said, a teasing smile on her face, but her eyes were wary.

"Will you marry me?" At her silence, he continued. "I need a wife and you need a husband and so I …"

"So you thought you would ask me, as I am bound to be desperate? After all, who would travel halfway across the country to marry a man she hadn't met?" Katie couldn't continue, the tears making her lose her voice.

Daniel stood and stared. What on earth just happened? He'd asked the women he loved to marry him and she thought he was trying to insult her.

"Katie, wait. I didn't mean it..."

"Go away, Daniel. I don't need your pity or anyone else's. I know what people are saying about me."

"Katie, I don't have a clue what you are talking about. All I care about is this. I love you and I want you to be my wife."

KATIE'S HEART SOARED. He loved her. All her dreams had come true. She could have her happily ever after. She looked up into his face and saw the love shining out of his eyes. Her legs melted and she had to grab the chair back to stop herself from falling over.

He as good as bought her. Mrs. Grey's horrible words rang through her head. Staying here with Daniel would ruin his life. He needed his neighbors to help him grow his business. He had to be honest, law abiding and free from all suspicion. Otherwise people wouldn't trade with him. He couldn't afford to be associated with a common... She couldn't bring herself to finish that thought.

A choked sob broke from her lips. She couldn't bear to live without him, yet she knew she must. He wouldn't entertain gossip. He would tell her to rise above it, that nobody would let a nasty rumor prevent them from shopping at a good store. Men were like that. They didn't credit women with much influence, but she knew better. In a household, it was usually the lady of the house who held the purse strings. The ladies of the town would follow Mrs. Grey's lead. His business would be destroyed. He would lose everything. Katie hung her head. She knew this time she was beat.

"I'm sorry, Daniel, but I don't feel the same about you." She stared at the floor, knowing if she looked at him, he would see her true feelings. "I have decided to take Ellen back to Ireland. As soon as I can make the money to cover the train fares, we are leaving for Boston."

It took every ounce of strength she possessed to walk out of the room and leave him behind. Once the door was closed, she ran to her room and, throwing herself on the bed, finally gave way to the tears.

DANIEL STOOD in the dining room, his shocked gaze on the closed door. Ireland? She had told him enough about what happened over there to know she had to be desperate to go back. He couldn't believe she didn't have feelings for him. Her response to his kiss had told him differently. He started to go after her and then stopped. Maybe it had all been too much for her. He should have given her more time to get over the events of the last week. It must have been a huge shock finding out you were about to marry into a family of thieving varmints. Reluctantly, he decided not to go after her. There were chores to do and they weren't going to wait for anyone.

CHAPTER 36

Katie stopped outside the kitchen door. Taking a deep breath, she pushed it open hoping he wouldn't be inside. He wasn't. She filled the kettle intent on making coffee. After the sleepless night, she needed something to keep her awake. Mrs. Sullivan appeared and the look she gave Katie made her heart sink.

"Why?"

Katie steeled herself to respond. "Why what?" She didn't look at the older woman but concentrated on making breakfast.

"Katie, I may be biased but Daniel is a good man. He's strong, healthy and thinks the world of you. I thought you had feelings for him too. It certainly appeared that way the other night."

Katie's cheeks burned. Mrs. Sullivan must have

seen their kiss. She swallowed hard. Should she explain?

"I'm sorry, Mrs. Sullivan, but it is best for everyone if we go home. To Galway."

Mrs. Sullivan spluttered. "To Ireland? I thought Daniel got that part wrong. You told me you wouldn't ever go back. There was nothing for you there. What's changed?" Mrs. Sullivan took the kettle out of Katie's shaking hands. "Come sit down. Tell me the truth. Why are you breaking my boy's heart?"

"I'm sorry. I can't explain. It is just for the best. I am not good for Daniel." Katie twisted a napkin in her hands. She couldn't look at Daniel's mother. "I've made a mess of everything. Coming out west was a mistake."

"Nonsense. Running away is the mistake. I thought more of you, Katie O'Callaghan. I may not have known you long but you struck me as someone who was brave, fearless and determined to stand by her loved ones. But at the first hint of trouble, you are running off home."

"I'm not running anywhere." Katie protested, sitting up straighter.

"Really? That's what it looks like from where I'm sitting." Mrs. Sullivan stood and looked down at Katie, her eyes filled with sadness. Her tone softened. "Trust me, Katie. You won't find happiness until you face your fears. Stand up for yourself. If you can't do it for yourself, do it for my son. He will lose everything he ever dreamed of and more if you get on that train."

Katie sat up straight until Mrs. Sullivan closed the door behind her. Then she let the tears fall as she laid her head on the table. She didn't want to hurt Daniel or his family but it was best she leave.

Other people's opinions are none of your business. Her mam's Irish lilt filled her head. She had always said that phrase if anyone had said anything bad about their family, particularly Liam. Her mam hadn't been prepared to walk away from her home to suit someone else.

She had been running since the day her Mam died. When would she stop? Maybe Mrs. Sullivan was right. It was time to make a stand. Her Mam had stood up to a regiment of soldiers. Mrs. Grey was only one woman.

Katie gulped down her coffee before heading to her room to change and do her hair more elegantly. She was going to show Mrs. Grey what Irish women were made of.

Mr. Brook was pleased to see her. He poured her a cup of coffee as she started cleaning the area she would work in. She had brought in two dresses to display her work, one a regular day dress but the second was the one that grabbed the women's attention. It may not have turned heads in Boston, but to the women of Clover Springs, it looked as if it had been imported from Paris. Mr. Brook introduced her to everyone, explaining she was from Boston where she had acquired vast experience as a seamstress. Katie wasn't sure she agreed with his description – after all she had only sewn a couple of dresses for her aunt but he convinced her it was all part of the sales routine. It worked. By the end of the first week, she had an order for a new dress, a shirt waist and more mending projects than she could expect to complete. The latter came from the steady stream of male customers. Mr. Brook smiled knowingly as one man after the other made a point of talking to Miss O'Callaghan personally.

The day flew by. Katie scarcely had time to think, let alone sit. Her feet ached by the time, Mr. Brook pulled the blind down and locked the door. It was good for her though, as it meant by the time she got back to the boarding house, she was so worn out she would sleep soundly. Well, most of the night anyway. Ellen wasn't speaking to her, being angry at the thought of leaving Clover Springs. Daniel hadn't come back. She guessed he was working out on Davy's ranch. She missed him dreadfully but she couldn't blame him for being angry.

. . .

DANIEL COULDN'T REMEMBER the last time he had worked so hard. But no matter how tired he got, he couldn't sleep. Images of Katie kept him awake. He was annoyed she had turned him down. He didn't understand why but it wasn't that keeping him awake. He had a feeling he had messed up somehow. That there was part of the puzzle he was missing. Did Katie want him to follow her to Ireland? Did she think that he wouldn't be prepared to live in Galway? True, he preferred to stay in Clover Springs but he wasn't going to lose Katie. He would follow her anywhere. He thought about going back to town to speak to her but his Ma had suggested he wait. She thought it would be good to give Katie time. She hadn't clarified what Katie was doing but his Ma knew more about women than he did. He had to trust her on this one but his patience was wearing thin.

CHAPTER 37

Everything was going so well, Katie started to think there was a chance she could stay in Clover Springs. She would have her own business and maybe with time, the man of her dreams. If he ever spoke to her again. Friday morning, the shop bell tinkled as another customer entered the store. She looked up with a smile only to come face to face with Mrs. Grey.

"It's true then. You are working here?"

Although phrased as a question, Katie guessed the woman didn't want an answer. She took a deep breath before speaking.

"Good morning, Mrs. Grey. Beautiful day, isn't it?" Katie noted the surprise in the other woman's eyes with satisfaction. *Take that you old bat.* She turned away slightly to compose herself.

"I don't need anything. I just wanted to see for myself. I can't believe you have the audacity to show yourself in public."

"I don't have anything to hide. I came to Colorado thinking I was getting married. That didn't work out. I have to provide for myself and Ellen so I took a job. I am using the talents God gave me to earn a decent living. What's wrong with that?"

Katie felt stronger as the other woman took a few seconds to reply. She isn't used to people talking back at her.

"Don't get too comfortable, Miss. I know your type and we don't need or want the likes of you in Clover Springs."

Katie couldn't help shaking at the venom directed at her. She watched silently as the older woman stalked out of the store. Then she sat down before her legs gave way.

It didn't take long before Mrs. Grey's influence became apparent. Dress orders were cancelled throughout the day on the flimsiest of excuses. Katie's hopes for the future dwindled. She thought she hid her disappointment well. She stuck a smile on her face as she helped Mr. Brook deal with regular mercantile customers.

As he locked up on Saturday evening, Mr. Brook insisted she take a seat and share a coffee and some cake with him. He wanted to celebrate record takings.

"I wish I had thought of employing someone like you sooner. It's amazing how many men required goods every day this week. Usually I see them once or twice a month." He smiled at Katie. "It won't be long before you have more marriage offers than you can shake a stick at. Best not let Daniel know, he will insist you leave."

"It's not Daniel I'm worried about." Katie wished she could swallow the words as soon as she said them. "Oh, is that the time? Mrs. Sullivan will have dinner waiting." Katie took her shawl from the back of the door but Mr. Brook wasn't going to let her get away that easily.

"Do you want to explain that comment or shall I guess?" When Katie didn't reply, he sighed. "Am I right in thinking you heard what Mrs. Grey has been saying?"

Katie nodded. "Aye, but she is only saying what others are thinking."

"Is that a fact? Do you know the people of Clover Springs that well?"

His sarcasm confused her. "Well, no, but surely they are like any small town. People gossip. You must have noticed that there haven't been any new orders for dresses and the ones I had were cancelled. All but one for Mrs. Murray, but I think Mrs. Sullivan is a close friend of hers."

"Yes, some gossip, but what is news today is history tomorrow. After everything you have been through, are you going to let one woman's actions change your destiny?"

"I don't know what that is anymore."

"Katie, you told me you came to America to find a new life. A better one where people mattered regardless of their background, their nationality or the color of their skin."

Katie nodded.

"So why are you letting one cranky old woman dictate how you live your life or, more to the point perhaps, mine?"

"How is Mrs. Grey running your life?"

"I am an old man, Katie. I don't know how much time I have left. " Katie tried to protest but he stopped her with a look. "I want to spend that time with my daughter and grandchildren. I can't do that unless I sell the store."

"Oh."

"I could sell to someone else. In fact, Mrs. Grey has expressed interest."

Katie didn't bother to hide her surprise. "What would she want with a store? I can't imagine her working behind the counter."

They exchanged looks before bursting into laughter at the idea. Then they fell silent.

"Power hungry people are everywhere. They don't have to be landed gentry or occupying forces to want control over people. Mrs. Grey is lonely and bored. Her children have grown up and left. What else can she do but meddle in things that don't concern her. Call me sentimental but I can't bear the thoughts of this place ending up in her hands." Mr. Brook stayed quiet for a couple of seconds but Katie didn't feel she could say anything. He sighed loudly. "But given the situation, I might have to take her offer."

"You can't do that. Then she's won. She's not going to give credit to Mrs. Kaufman or allow Mrs. Landers to pay off her bill with eggs and milk."

"What do you suggest I do? Work here until I die? Hold on for Daniel to raise the cash he needs?"

Katie realized too late what Mr. Brook was trying to do. She stood, her tone reflecting the regret in her eyes. "I'm really sorry, Mr. Brook. You deserve to go live with your family. You are a lovely man but I can't help you."

"Can't or won't, Katie?"

Katie didn't answer but closed the door quietly behind her. His question rang in her ears the whole way home.

CHAPTER 38

She stood looking around the kitchen thinking how much she would miss it. The boarding house was a real home not like her Uncle's mansion in Boston.

Parting from Daddy had been bad, but leaving here would be worse. She loved Daniel with every fiber of her being, but she had to leave. Despite what Mr. Brook and Mrs. Sullivan thought, it was for the best. She didn't like letting Mrs. Grey win, but it wasn't her future on the line. She couldn't risk Daniel getting caught in the crossfire.

Katie jumped at the sound of the door banging. *Please don't let it be him.*

"There you are. I've been looking everywhere for you" Daniel looked at her, but the question in his eyes made her stare at the floor. He reached out to take her hand. "I've missed you. Marry me, Katie."

The heat of his touch seared her whole body while his words made her heart want to leap out of her chest. *Yes,* her heart answered, but she couldn't say the words. Her head knew it was wrong. She loved him too much.

She jerked her hand from his and stood back slightly, trying to put as much distance between them as possible.

"I can't stay, Daniel."

"Okay. Then marry me and I will go with you to Ireland. " He leaned in toward her.

"Ireland? You can't do that. Your ma would be devastated. Besides, you love it here."

"I love you, Katie O'Callaghan. Where you go, I go."

"Don't make this harder. Please." Katie swallowed hard. Was he serious about leaving?

"Katie, I'm not the one being ornery." He moved closer, gripping her upper arms, bringing his head down toward hers. She gazed at his lips drawing closer and closed her eyes. *Just one more kiss couldn't hurt.*

The kiss was fierce, more savage than any other kiss they had shared. It was as if he was marking her his, yet behind it she sensed his desperation to prove he loved her. She yielded to him, showing him just how much she shared his feelings. After a few minutes, they broke apart, both breathing heavily.

"You can't leave me now, Katie."

"I have to. Don't you see? If I stay, I will ruin your life."

He pulled her closer, cupping her face in his hands, forcing her to look at him. "Losing you will ruin my life. If you leave, I will follow you. I won't let you go."

"Mrs. Grey said..."

Daniel cursed. "Sorry, but what has this got to do with her? I love you and you love me. Don't you?"

She couldn't lie, not when she was looking into his eyes. She tried to escape, but his grip tightened. With a sigh, she gave up. "Yes, I love you. More than anything in this world."

"Yes. Now you just have to marry me. Then we can have the future we deserve and Mrs. Grey can ..."

"Daniel!"

"Sorry, but that woman would try the patience of God himself."

Katie giggled before looking up into his eyes. "Kiss me again please."

"With pleasure, Ma'am." He bent his head, his lips teasing hers. She thought she would burst with happiness.

After a few minutes, she finally came up for air. "Daniel, I don't want to leave Clover Springs."

"That's good as neither do I. I'd miss Ma's cooking."

Katie poked him in the ribs but couldn't resist laughing too.

"I love you, Daniel Sullivan."

CHAPTER 39

Katie strove to calm her stomach that churned like a new batch of butter. Her hands fluttered over the new dress. It fit her like a glove. She never owned anything as beautiful before. She couldn't stop admiring her reflection even though vanity was a sin.

"You look beautiful, Katie." Ellen said softly, her eyes shimmering with unshed tears.

"You do, too." Katie gave her sister a hug, not caring if her dress got a little wrinkled. She couldn't bear it if her sister starting crying. She wouldn't be able to hold the tears back much longer herself.

There was a knock at the door and Mrs. Sullivan entered.

"Oh my word, aren't you as pretty as a picture."

"Thank you so much for the lending of your dress. It fits perfectly."

Mrs. Sullivan took Katie's hands in hers. Her husky tone suggested she too was struggling not to give in to the waterworks. "I hope you are as happy in your marriage as I was in mine. Daniel is a good man. He will make a fine husband, and you, my darling girl, will make him the best wife ever."

"Do you really believe that? What about what Mrs. Grey said?"

A stony look marred Mrs. Sullivan's pretty face. "You leave that old crone for me to deal with. May God forgive me, but I might just indulge my wish to give her a good slap one of these fine days."

Katie and Ellen laughed aloud at the idea of Mrs. Sullivan slapping anyone, least of all another fine upstanding member of the small Clover Springs community.

"Now, Ellen, are you going to tell Katie or shall I?"

"Tell me what?" Katie's mouth tightened with concern for her sister. Ellen's eyes were full of mischief. "What?"

Katie tried to keep her tone low, but she was getting frustrated. *She can't be upset or worried while her eyes are dancing in her head like that.*

"Come on now, girls. The men are waiting. Ellen, tell your sister and let's be off."

. . .

Katie looked at Ellen, her stomach churning even more. She couldn't help worrying, despite the mischievous look Ellen exchanged with Mrs. Sullivan.

"I'm not coming with you to the store. I am staying here with Mrs. Sullivan."

Katie opened her mouth to protest, but the look on her sister's face stopped her. "Katie, you have always put other people first. Now is your time for happiness. You and Daniel deserve to start your life together alone. You don't want your sister ruining all those romantic evenings. Mrs. Sullivan needs some help in the boarding house and I will be able to go back to school during the day. It's the ideal solution for everyone."

Katie hugged Ellen first and then Mrs. Sullivan. "I am so lucky to have both of you in my life. Thank you, Mrs. Sullivan."

"Katie, do you think you could stop calling me Mrs. Sullivan and start calling me Ma like Daniel does?"

"Yes, Ma." Katie smiled as the two women left the room.

Katie glanced once more in the mirror. She imagined she could see her mother at her shoulder smiling at her. "I will be happy, Mam. Just you see."

She left the boarding house. "Please let me walk

you." Daniel's brother, Davy, smiled before turning Katie toward the church. "Reverend Timmons came last night to say Father Cleary was in town. He is going to marry you."

Katie's step faltered. *Mam, you sent the priest, didn't you? It was your way to give us your blessing.* She looked up to the sky feeling a wave of love sweeping through her body. Her knees buckled as her nerves tingled with emotion. Davy's arm at her side helped her walk the couple of steps up and into the building.

The familiar smell of incense brought her immediately back to her childhood and memories of herself, Liam, and the rest of her family heading into church. She struggled but failed to stop the tears flowing. She wished she was in Galway with Daddy beside her to give her away. *But then you wouldn't have met Daniel.* He was her future.

Through the mist of the tears and her veil, she saw the figure of Daniel and his attendants at the top of the church. Ellen and Mrs. Sullivan took their places in the front pews. A few of the inhabitants of Clover Springs were also present. Katie barely noticed. Daniel had turned to look as she made her way toward the top of the Church. She looked at him, relieved to see her own feelings reflected in the way he gazed at her.

"Dearly beloved..."

Katie didn't hear the words of the service. She was

so caught up in her emotions, Daniel had to press her hand to remind her to say her vows.

She tensed when he asked the congregation if there was any reason why they could not be wed. *This was it.* Now her bubble of happiness would burst. But nothing happened. Before she knew it, the priest had announced that Daniel should kiss his bride. She almost exploded with happiness. They were married. At last.

She shivered as goose bumps appeared all over her body as Daniel gently removed the veil and leaned forward for their first kiss as man and wife. His lips were soft but insistent. *Later,* the kiss promised. She smiled, nodding slightly. His eyes darkened with desire, causing her legs to weaken. She wished they were alone and not in God's house so he could kiss her properly.

All too soon, it was over, and taking her hand, her new husband walked her out of the church and toward their new life. Together.

EPILOGUE

CLOVER SPRINGS, EIGHT MONTHS LATER

Katie rubbed her bump as the baby kicked her again. She waddled over to the rocking chair, glad to take the weight off her feet for a few minutes. She picked up the letter, wondering what Mary had thought of her suggestion.

She smiled in delight before calling out to Daniel. He came running up the stairs from their store. "What's wrong? Is it the baby?"

"No, darling. It's way too early yet." She waved the letter at him, feeling a little guilty for causing the worried frown on his face. She didn't know who was more nervous about the upcoming birth, her or Daniel.

"Mary Ryan said yes. She is coming to Clover Springs. Catherine is happy with her new family, so

Mary thinks it is time she moved on with her life. I hope she likes Davy."

"Everyone likes Davy. He's almost as nice as me." Daniel smiled down at his wife. "It was a great idea you had to act as a referee for the men in town for Mrs. Gantley. At least none of her other brides will arrive in town ready to marry a murderer."

"Oh, you. Mr. Cassidy wasn't a murderer." Katie pushed her finger into her husband's stomach. "Remember, if it wasn't for that varmint writing for a bride, I wouldn't be here."

Daniel stroked his chin. "True, I must remember to send him a Christmas gift to say thank you. I believe they don't get many of them in the Texan jail he now calls home."

Katie shivered. Despite the fact that Daniel was joking, it was still a rather touchy subject. She would never forget just how close she came to danger. At night, she often woke up drenched in sweat, having dreamt Virgil Cassidy was nearby. He had been hung shortly after their wedding. Montis had been sentenced to five years hard labor for living off the proceeds of the crime.

After the publicity of the trial, more people were aware she had come to Clover Springs as a mail order bride. Rather than look down on her, the townsfolk had been overcome with curiosity. A number of the men had approached her or Daniel asking if she could help them find brides. At Daniel's suggestion, she had written to Mrs. Gantley, offering to be a referee for the men from Clover Springs. Mrs. Gantley, after apologizing for the danger she had unwittingly placed Katie in, agreed with her suggestion. Between the two of them they had already arranged for a couple of mail order weddings to be held in Clover Springs. Now it was the turn of her brother-in-law and her best friend. She hoped Mary would like Clover Springs as much as she did. The town was special. It was home.

THANK you so much for reading Katie. I hope you want to continue reading about her and her friends in Clover Springs. Mary, the next book brings back old friends and introduces new ones.

ALSO BY RACHEL WESSON

The Resistance Sisters

Darkness Falls

Light Rises

Hearts at War

When's Mummy Coming

A Mother's Promise

WWII Irish Stand Alone

Stolen from her Mother

Orphans of Hope House

Home for unloved Orphans (Orphans of Hope House 1)

Baby on the Doorstep (Orphans of Hope House 2)

Women and War

Gracie under Fire

Penny's Secret Mission

Molly's Flight

Hearts on the Rails

Orphan Train Escape

Orphan Train Trials

Orphan Train Christmas

Orphan Train Tragedy

Orphan Train Strike

Orphan Train Disaster

Trail of Hearts - Oregon Trail Series

Oregon Bound (book 1)

Oregon Dreams (book 2)

Oregon Destiny (book 3)

Oregon Discovery (book 4)

Oregon Disaster (book 5)

12 Days of Christmas - co -authored series.

The Maid - book 8

Clover Springs Mail Order Brides

Katie (Book 1)

Mary (Book 2)

Sorcha (Book 3)

Emer (Book 4)

Laura (Book 5)

Ellen (Book 6)

Thanksgiving in Clover Springs (book 7)

Christmas in Clover Springs (book8)

Erin (Book 9)

Eleanor (book 10)

Cathy (book 11)

Mrs. Grey

Clover Springs East

New York Bound (book 1)

New York Storm (book 2)

New York Hope (book 3)

ACKNOWLEDGMENTS

This book wouldn't have been possible without the help of so many people. Thanks to Erin Dameron-Hill for my fantastic covers. Erin is a gifted artist who makes my characters come to life.

Special thanks go to Nancy Cowan, Marlene Larsen, Cindy Nipper, Marilyn Cortellini, Sherry Masters, Janet Lessley, Robin Malek, Meisje Sanders Arcuri and Denise Cervantes who all spotted errors (mine) that had slipped through.

Come join us at https://www.facebook.com/groups/rachelwessonsreaders

Last, but by no means least, huge thanks and love to my husband and my three children.

Made in the USA
Middletown, DE
27 August 2024